DISNEY

TIM BURTON'S THE NIGHTMARE BEFORE CHRISTMAS

THE STORY OF THE MOVIE IN COMICS

Dark Horse Books

JACK SKELLINGTON

JACK SKELLINGTON, THE TALL AND THIN PUMPKIN KING OF HALLOWEEN TOWN, IS A TERRIFYING SKELETON THAT WOULD CHILL THE BRAVEST MEN WITH A SIMPLE WHISPER. BUT DESPITE HIS BLOODCURDLING SMILE, JACK IS GENTLE, KIND, AND PATIENT AT HEART. AND HE WANTS MORE THAN JUST TO FRIGHTEN PEOPLE. LONELY AND MELANCHOLY, JACK IS LOOKING FOR SOMETHING NEW, SOMETHING OTHER THAN THE USUAL HALLOWEEN NIGHT . . .

ZERO

JACK'S LOYAL AND PLAYFUL GHOST DOG IS NEVER FAR FROM HIM. ZERO USUALLY SPENDS MOST OF THE DAY SLEEPING AT HOME OR AT THE CEMETERY, BUT HE IS ALWAYS READY TO FOLLOW JACK FOR A WALK OR TO PLAY CATCH WITH JACK'S RIBS. ALTHOUGH HE MAY NOT ALWAYS UNDERSTAND HIS OWNER'S INTENTIONS, ZERO IS ALWAYS READY TO HELP.

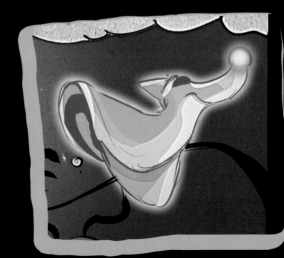

SALLY

CREATED BY DR. FINKLESTEIN, SALLY IS A RAG DOLL MADE OF DIFFERENT PIECES STITCHED TOGETHER AND STUFFED WITH AUTUMN LEAVES. EACH PIECE HAS A LIFE OF ITS OWN, AND CAN DETACH AND MOVE INDEPENDENTLY, SO SALLY CAN ALWAYS PUT HERSELF BACK TOGETHER AGAIN WITH A NEEDLE AND THREAD. RESOURCEFUL AND BRAVE, SALLY IS JACK'S TRUEST FRIEND. LIKE HIM, SHE YEARNS FOR SOMETHING ELSE FROM LIFE.

SANTA CLAUS

JOLLY AND CARING, SANTA CLAUS IS THE RULER OF CHRISTMAS TOWN AND, LIKE JACK, WORKS ALL YEAR TO PREPARE FOR ONE NIGHT. EVERYTHING ABOUT HIM FASCINATES THE PUMPKIN KING, ESPECIALLY HIS NAME—WHICH JACK ACTUALLY MISHEARS AS SANDY CLAWS! DESPITE HIS BIG BUILD, SANTA CLAUS CAN EASILY GET THROUGH NARROW SPACES LIKE THE CHIMNEYS OF MOST HOUSES.

THE MAYOR

VERBOSE, INSECURE, AND BADLY EQUIPPED TO HANDLE EMERGENCIES, THE MAYOR OF HALLOWEEN TOWN CANNOT MAKE ANY DECISION ALONE—NOT EVEN THE EASIEST ONES, LIKE PLANNING THE NEXT HALLOWEEN. HE IS LITERALLY TWOFACED: WHEN HE IS HAPPY, THE MAYOR SHOWS A SMILEY FACE, AND WHEN HE IS WORRIED, HIS HEAD TURNS AND DISPLAYS A QUITE CONCERNED EXPRESSION.

DR. FINKLESTEIN

THE EVIL SCIENTIST OF HALLOWEEN TOWN AND A WELL-KNOWN GENIUS, DR. FINKLESTEIN IS THE CREATOR OF SALLY AND CONSIDERS HER HIS BEST AND MOST PRECIOUS WORK. IT IS FOR THIS REASON THAT FINKLESTEIN HOLDS HER PRISONER—UNSUCCESSFULLY, MOST OF THE TIME—IN HIS HOUSE. FINKLESTEIN'S HEAD IS A METAL PLATE AND HE CAN OPEN IT TO RUB HIS BRAIN WHEN HE NEEDS TO FOCUS ON SOMETHING.

OOGIE BOOGIE

HIS LAIR IS A STRANGE AND SPOOKY GAMBLING DEN, LIT UP WITH ULTRAVIOLET LIGHTS AND FILLED WITH TORTURE DEVICES. MR. OOGIE BOOGIE'S BODY IS MADE OF COUNTLESS CREEPY BUGS CONTAINED IN A BURLAP SACK, AND HIS SOUL IS JUST AS SINISTER. OOGIE BOOGIE IS THE ULTIMATE NIGHTMARE—THE MEANEST, MOST EVIL CITIZEN OF HALLOWEEN TOWN AND ITS ONLY TRUE VILLAIN. HE ONLY FEARS JACK SKELLINGTON; AND HE LOVES GAMBLING, BUT HE HAS NO SKILL FOR IT AND CHEATS MOST OF THE TIME!

LOCK, SHOCK & BARREL

THE BEST TRICK-OR-TREATERS IN HALLOWEEN TOWN, THESE THREE MISCHIEVOUS LITTLE DEMONS TRAVEL AROUND IN A WALKING BATHTUB AND LIVE IN A TREEHOUSE OUTSIDE THE CITY, JUST ABOVE MR. OOGIE BOOGIE'S LAIR. THEY USUALLY WORK FOR OOGIE BOOGIE, BUT OCCASIONALLY THEY'LL ACCEPT A JOB FROM JACK SKELLINGTON. THEY ALL WEAR MASKS: LOCK WEARS A DEVIL MASK; SHOCK, A WITCH MASK; AND BARREL, A GHOUL MASK. BUT STRANGELY ENOUGH, THEIR FACES LOOK EXACTLY LIKE THEIR MASKS!

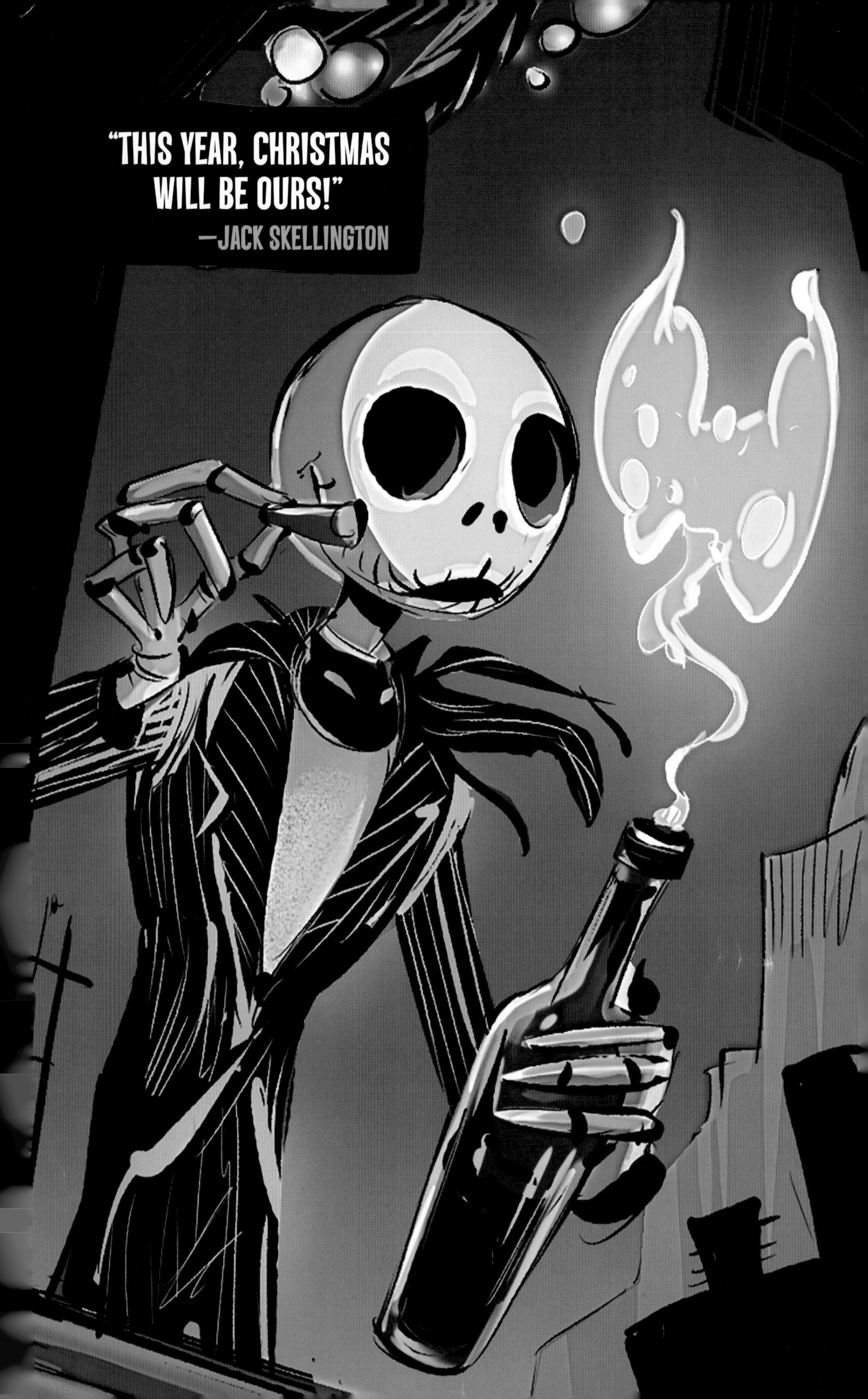
"THIS YEAR, CHRISTMAS
WILL BE OURS!"
—JACK SKELLINGTON

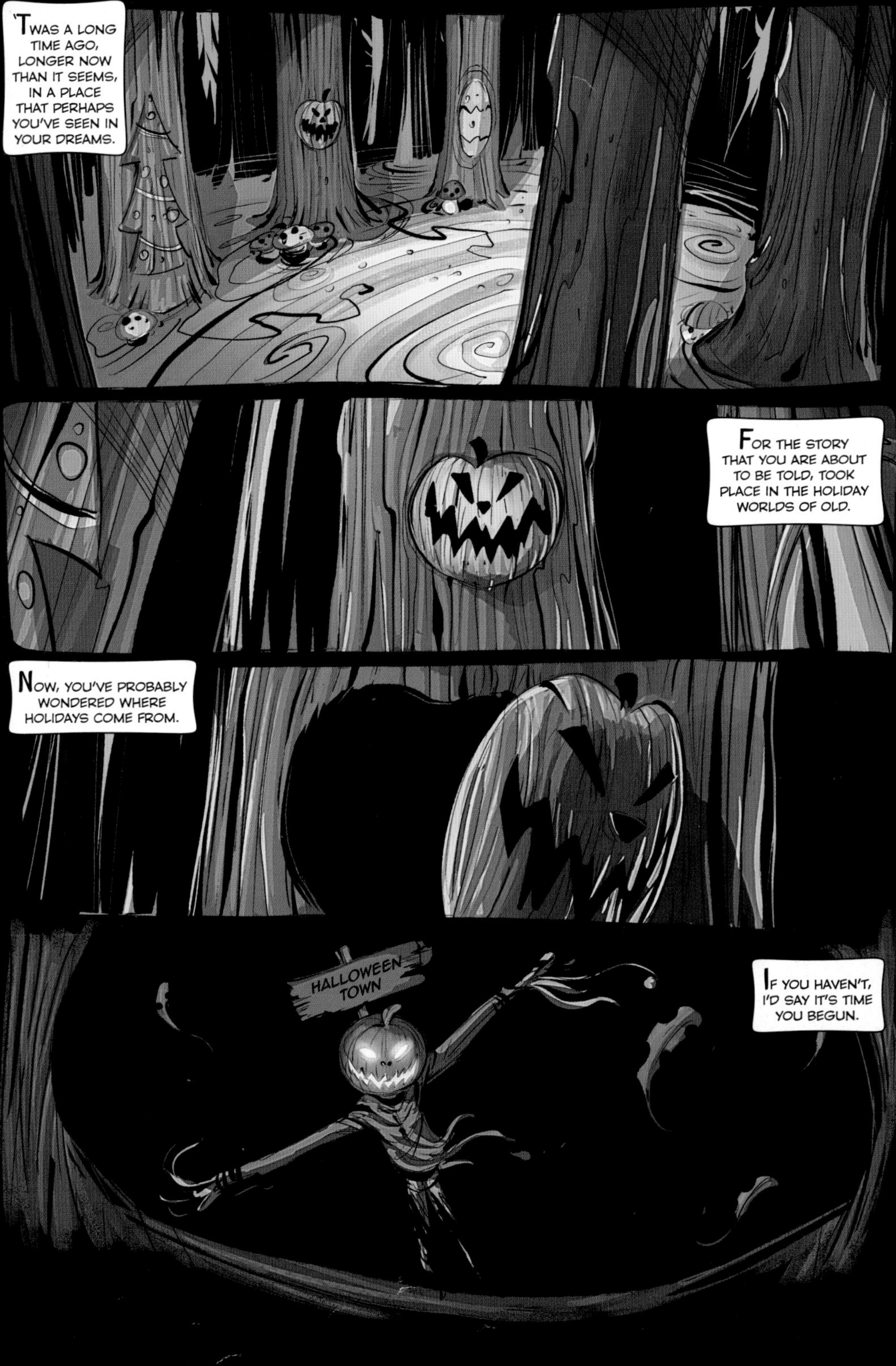
'Twas a long time ago, longer now than it seems, in a place that perhaps you've seen in your dreams.
For the story that you are about to be told, took place in the holiday worlds of old.
Now, you've probably wondered where holidays come from.
Halloween Town
If you haven't, I'd say it's time you begun.

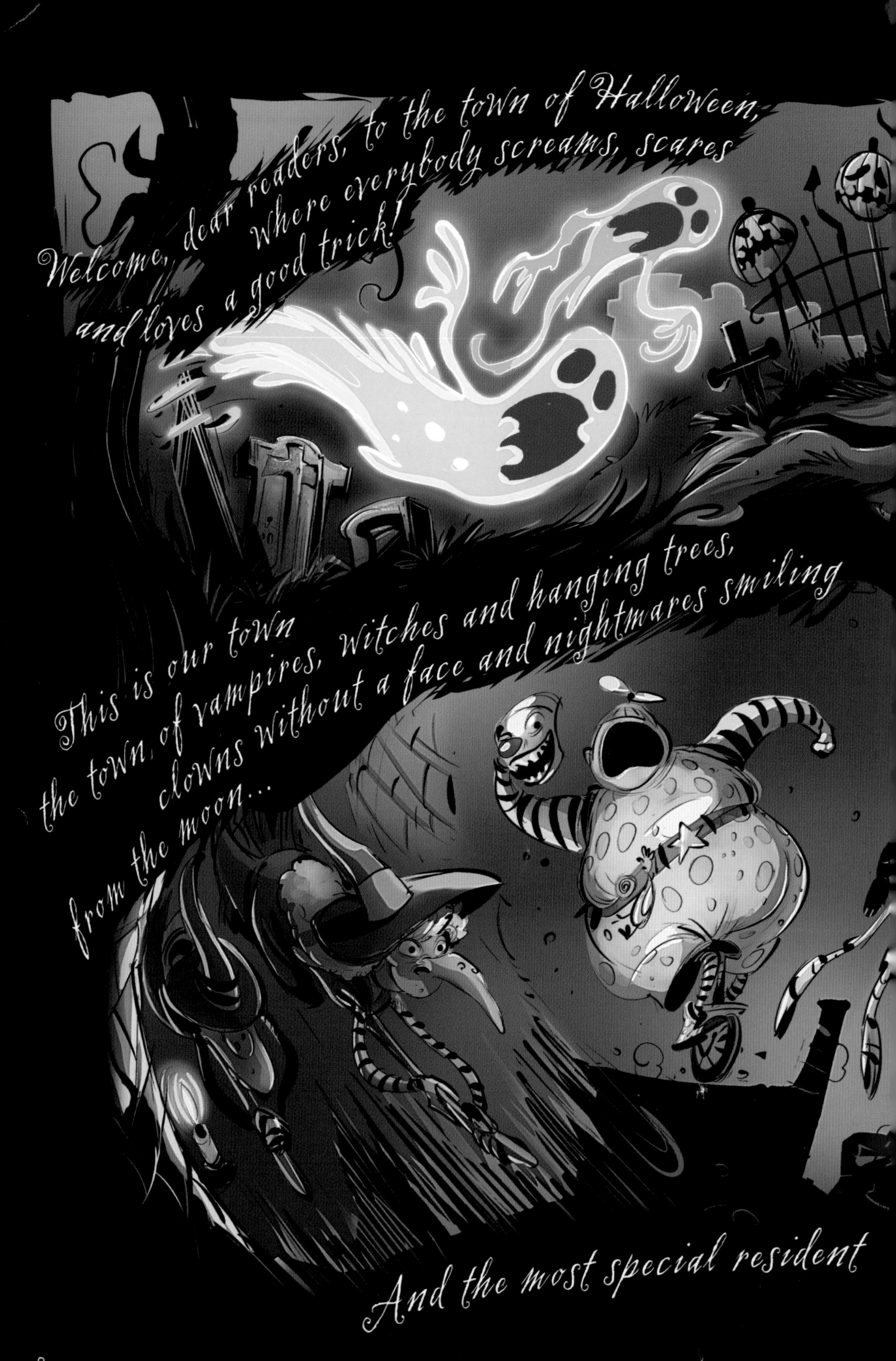
Welcome, dear readers, to the town of Halloween,
where everybody screams, scares
and loves a good trick!
This is our town
the town of vampires, witches and hanging trees,
clowns without a face and nightmares smiling
from the moon...
And the most special resident

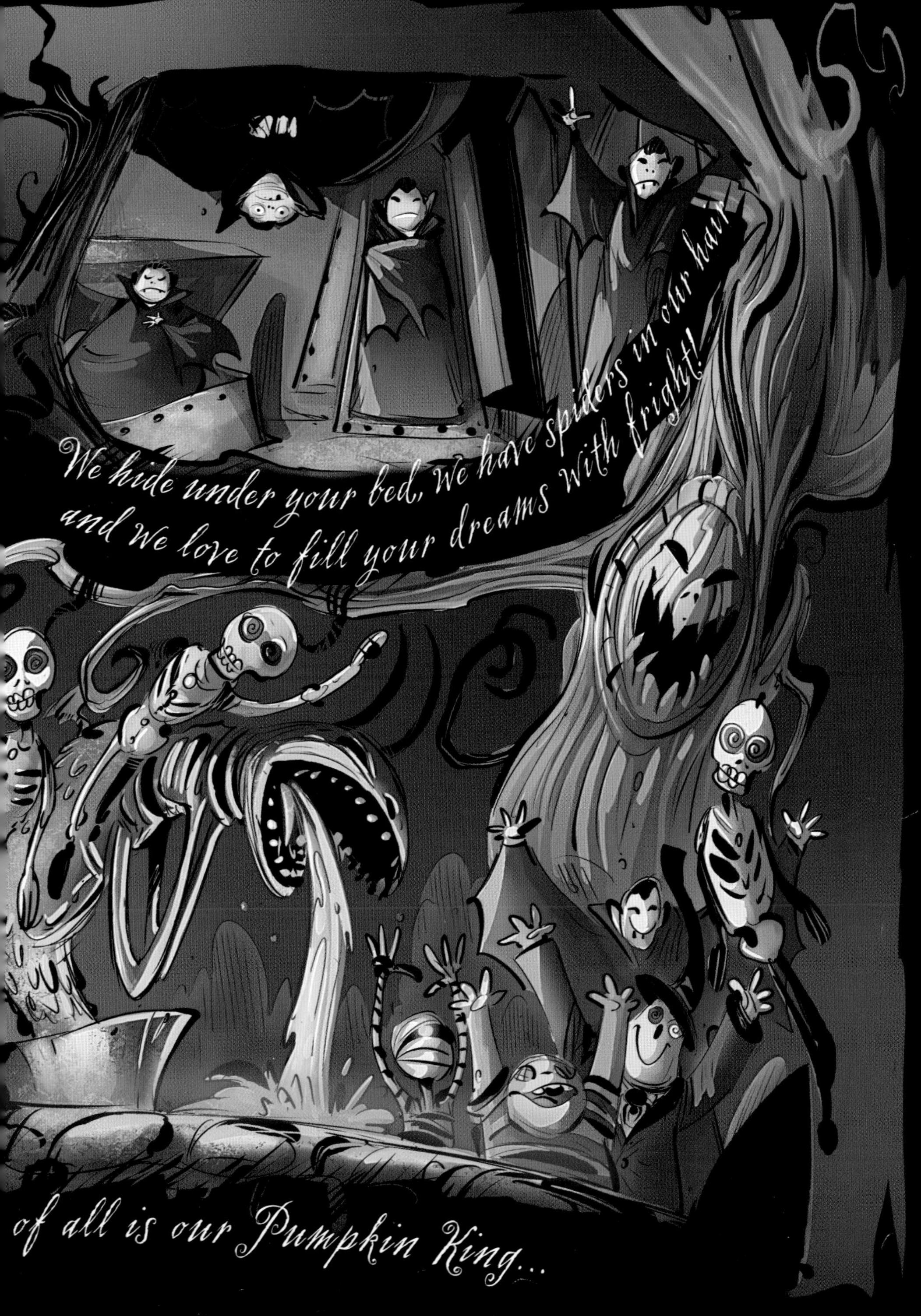

We hide under your bed, we have spiders in our hair
and we love to fill your dreams with fright!

of all is our Pumpkin King...

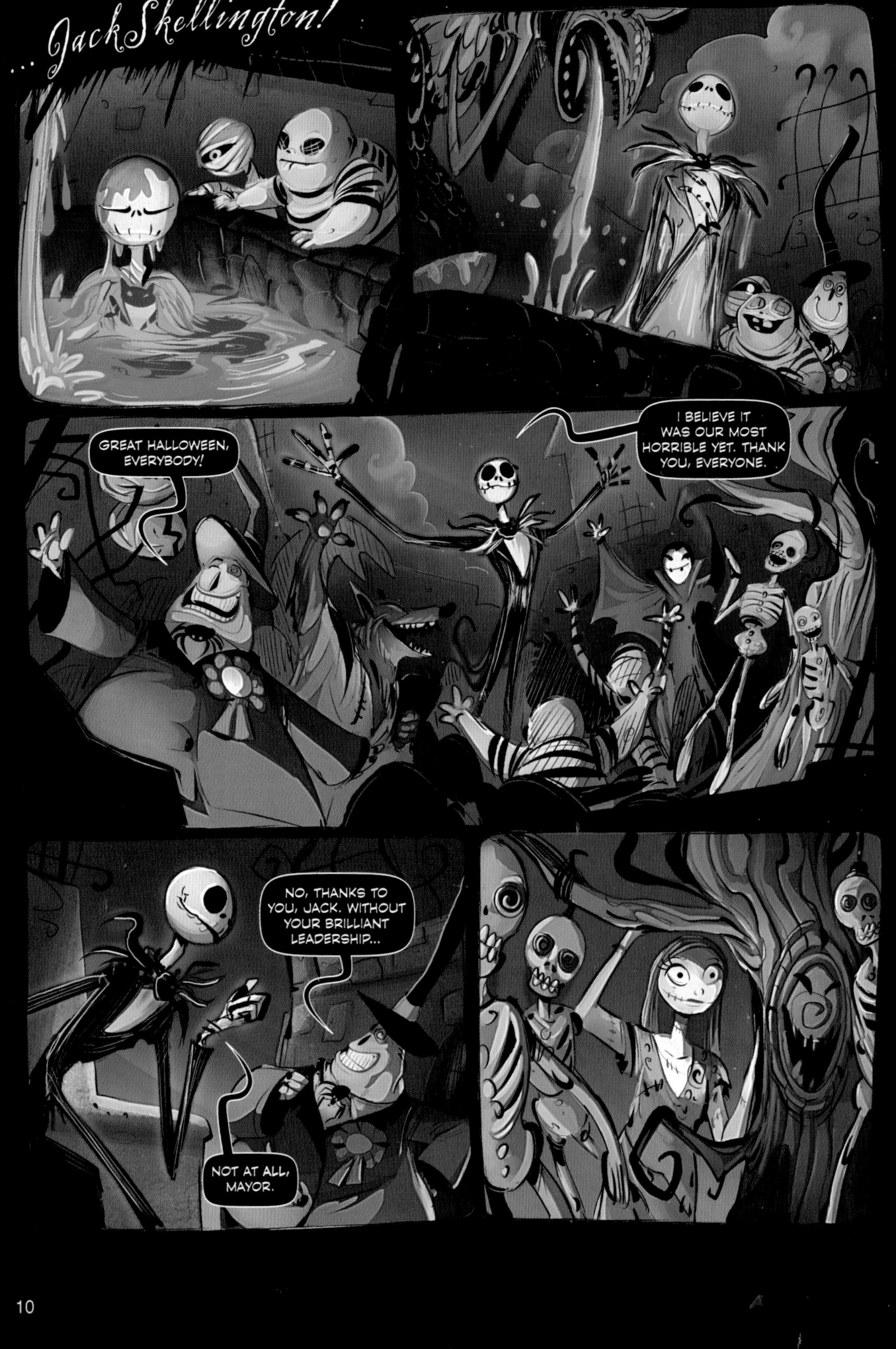

...Jack Skellington!
GREAT HALLOWEEN, EVERYBODY!
I BELIEVE IT WAS OUR MOST HORRIBLE YET. THANK YOU, EVERYONE.
NO, THANKS TO YOU, JACK. WITHOUT YOUR BRILLIANT LEADERSHIP...
NOT AT ALL, MAYOR.

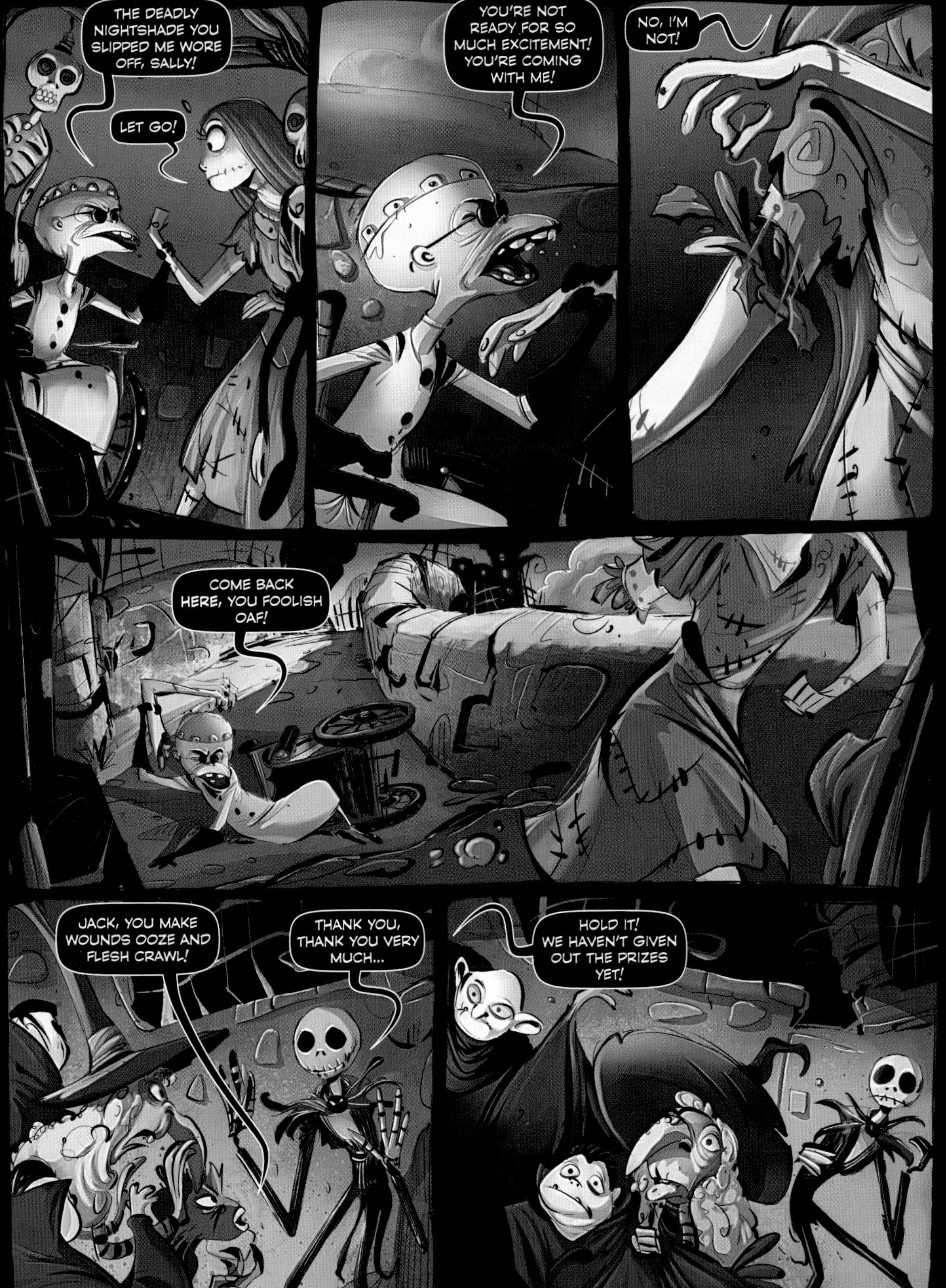
THE DEADLY NIGHTSHADE YOU SLIPPED ME WORE OFF, SALLY!
LET GO!
YOU'RE NOT READY FOR SO MUCH EXCITEMENT! YOU'RE COMING WITH ME!
NO, I'M NOT!
COME BACK HERE, YOU FOOLISH OAF!
JACK, YOU MAKE WOUNDS OOZE AND FLESH CRAWL!
THANK YOU, THANK YOU VERY MUCH...
HOLD IT! WE HAVEN'T GIVEN OUT THE PRIZES YET!

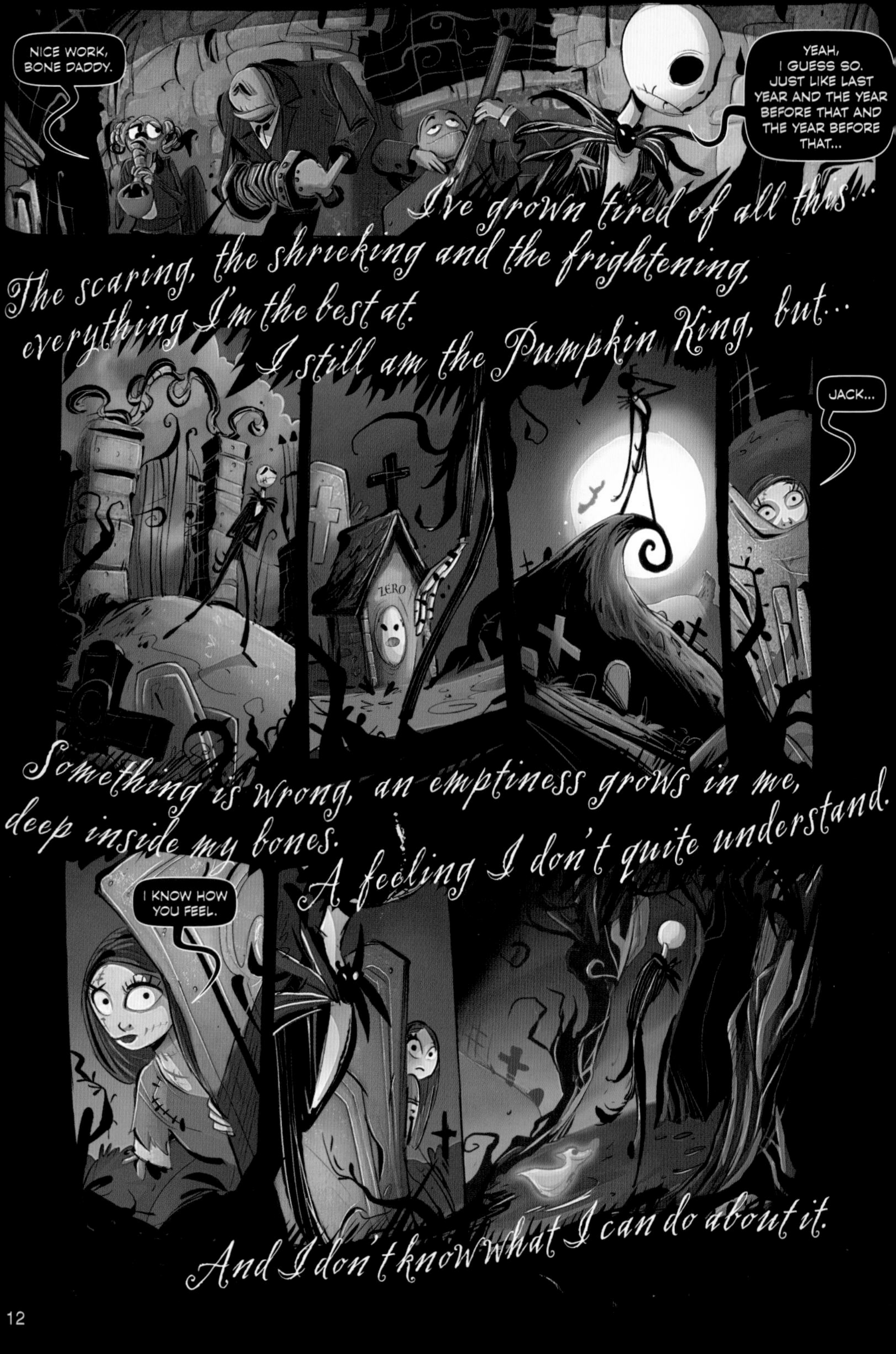
NICE WORK, BONE DADDY.
YEAH, I GUESS SO. JUST LIKE LAST YEAR AND THE YEAR BEFORE THAT AND THE YEAR BEFORE THAT...
I've grown tired of all this...
The scaring, the shrieking and the frightening, everything I'm the best at.
I still am the Pumpkin King, but...
ZERO
JACK...
Something is wrong, an emptiness grows in me, deep inside my bones.
A feeling I don't quite understand.
I KNOW HOW YOU FEEL.
And I don't know what I can do about it.

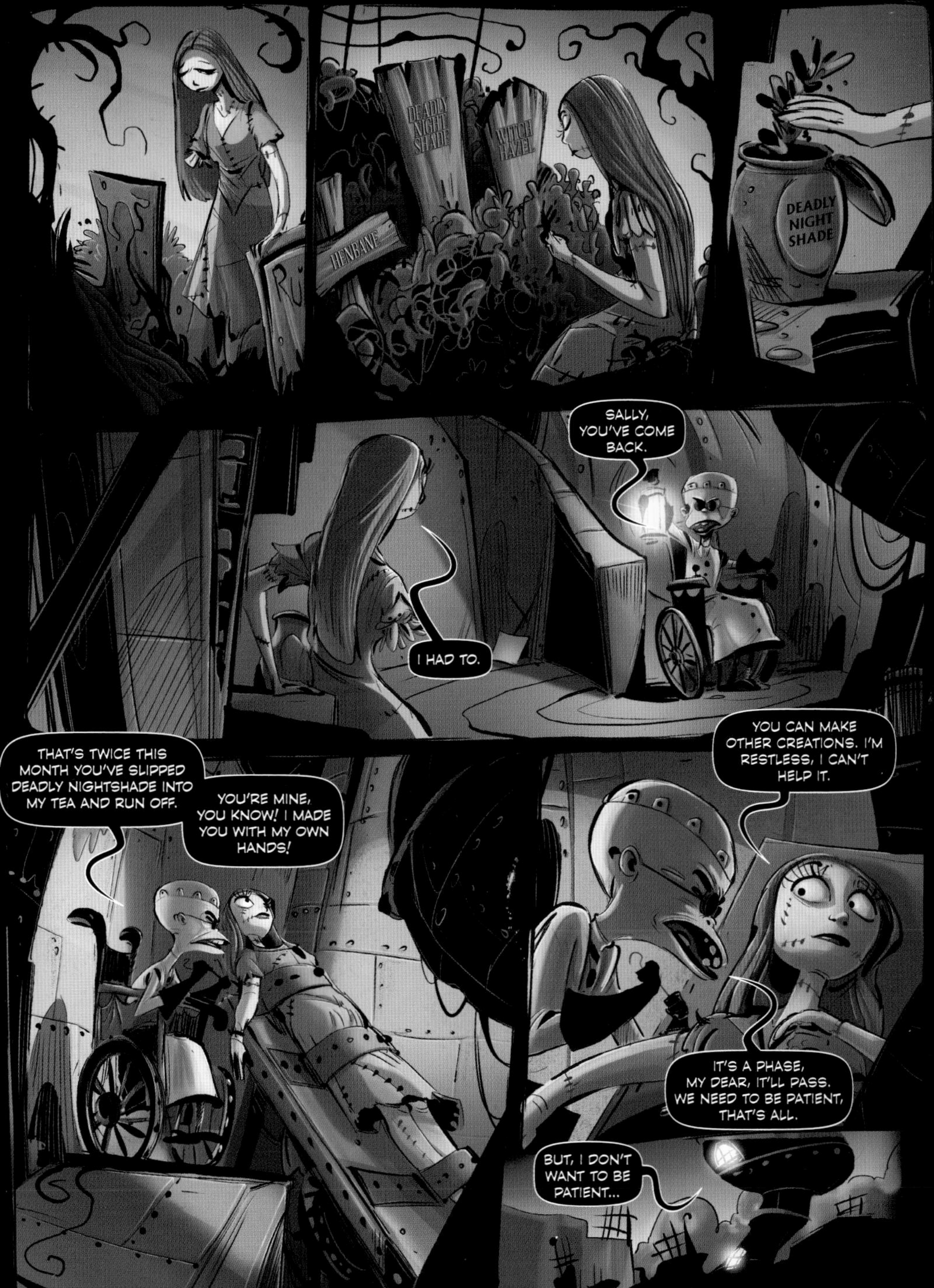
DEADLY NIGHT SHADE
WITCH HAZEL
HENBANE
DEADLY NIGHT SHADE
SALLY, YOU'VE COME BACK.
I HAD TO.
THAT'S TWICE THIS MONTH YOU'VE SLIPPED DEADLY NIGHTSHADE INTO MY TEA AND RUN OFF.
YOU'RE MINE, YOU KNOW! I MADE YOU WITH MY OWN HANDS!
YOU CAN MAKE OTHER CREATIONS. I'M RESTLESS, I CAN'T HELP IT.
IT'S A PHASE, MY DEAR, IT'LL PASS. WE NEED TO BE PATIENT, THAT'S ALL.
BUT, I DON'T WANT TO BE PATIENT...

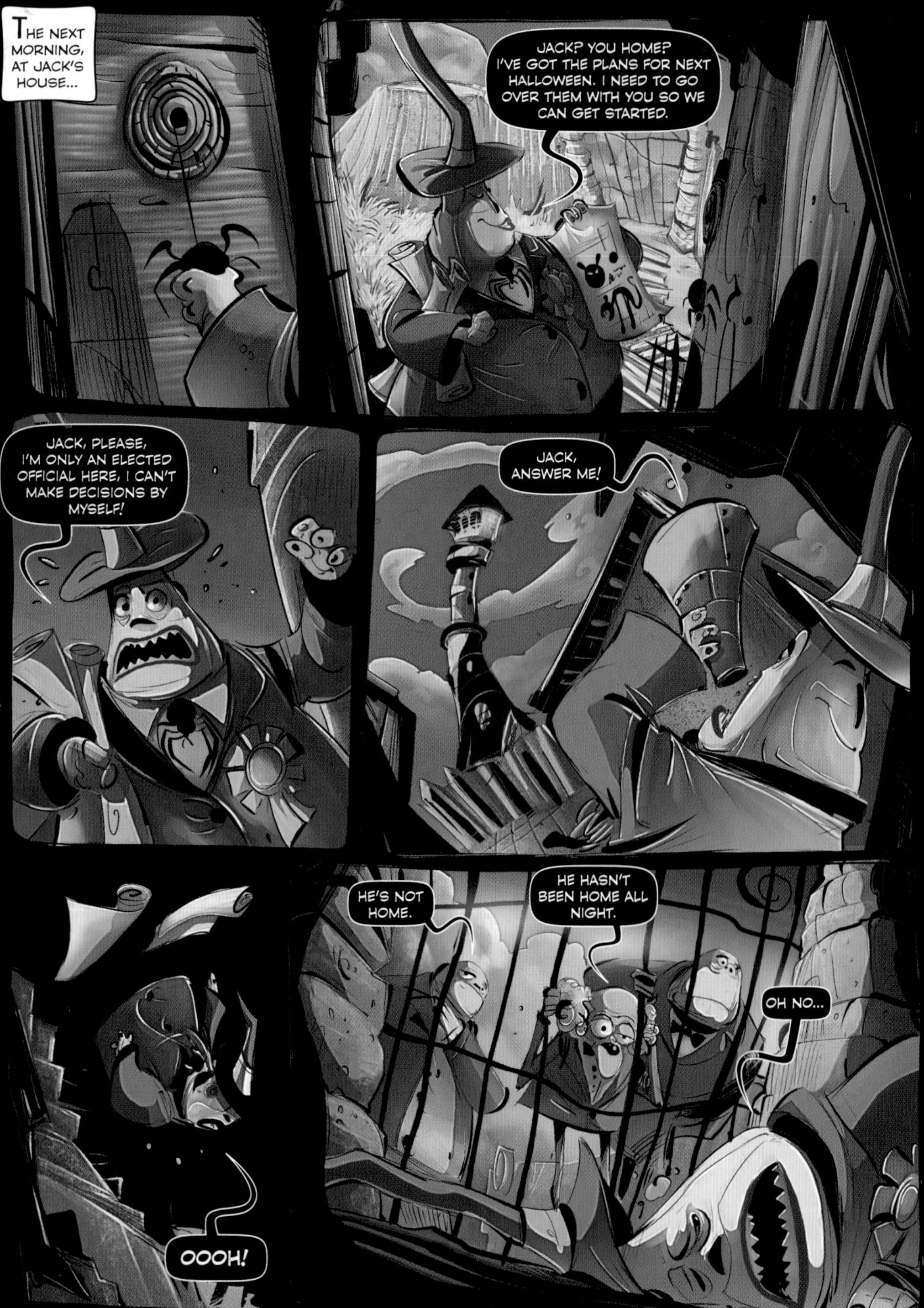
THE NEXT MORNING, AT JACK'S HOUSE...
JACK? YOU HOME? I'VE GOT THE PLANS FOR NEXT HALLOWEEN. I NEED TO GO OVER THEM WITH YOU SO WE CAN GET STARTED.
JACK, PLEASE, I'M ONLY AN ELECTED OFFICIAL HERE, I CAN'T MAKE DECISIONS BY MYSELF!
JACK, ANSWER ME!
OOOH!
HE'S NOT HOME.
HE HASN'T BEEN HOME ALL NIGHT.
OH NO...

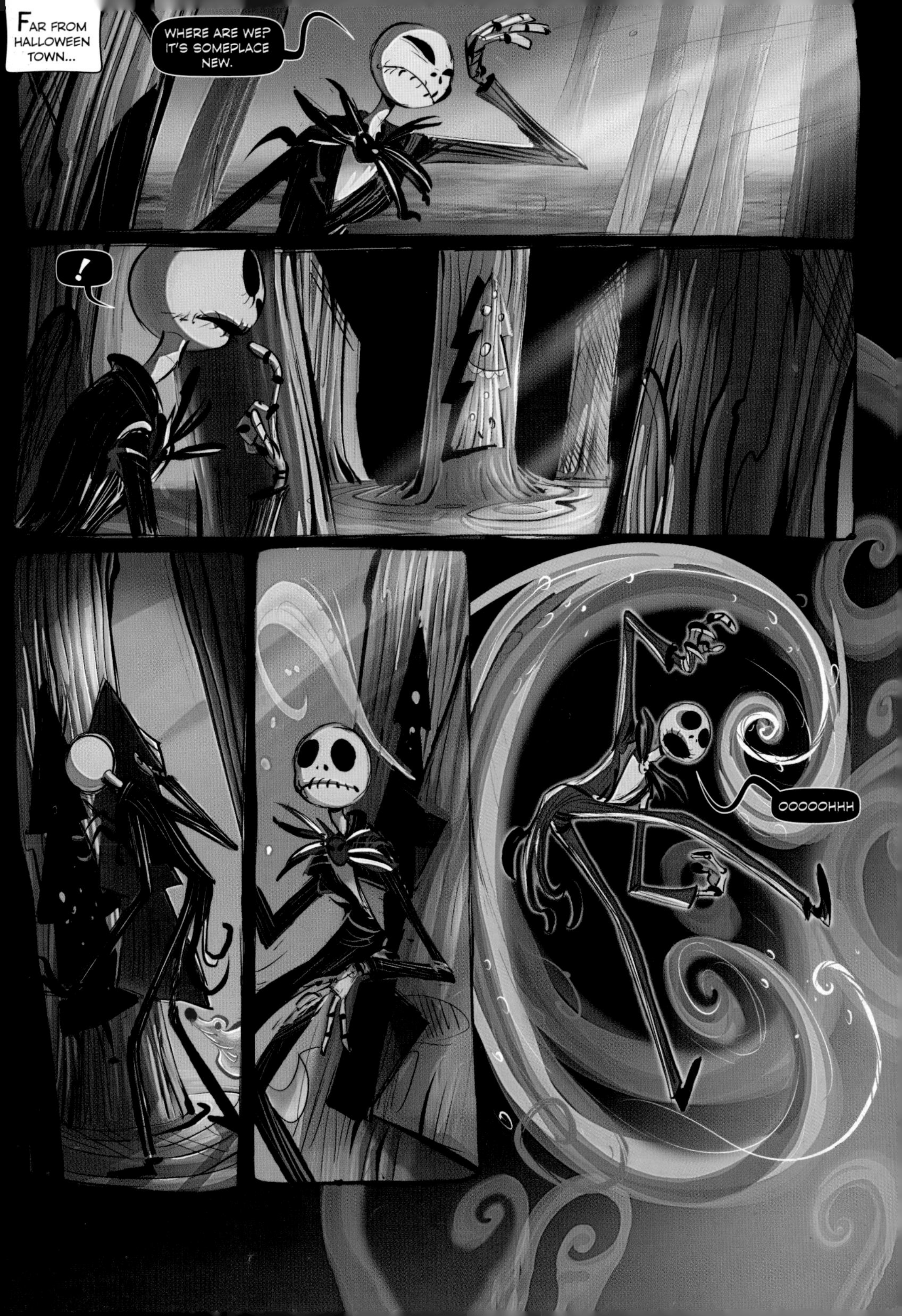
Far from Halloween Town...
Where are we? It's someplace new.
!
OOOOOHHH

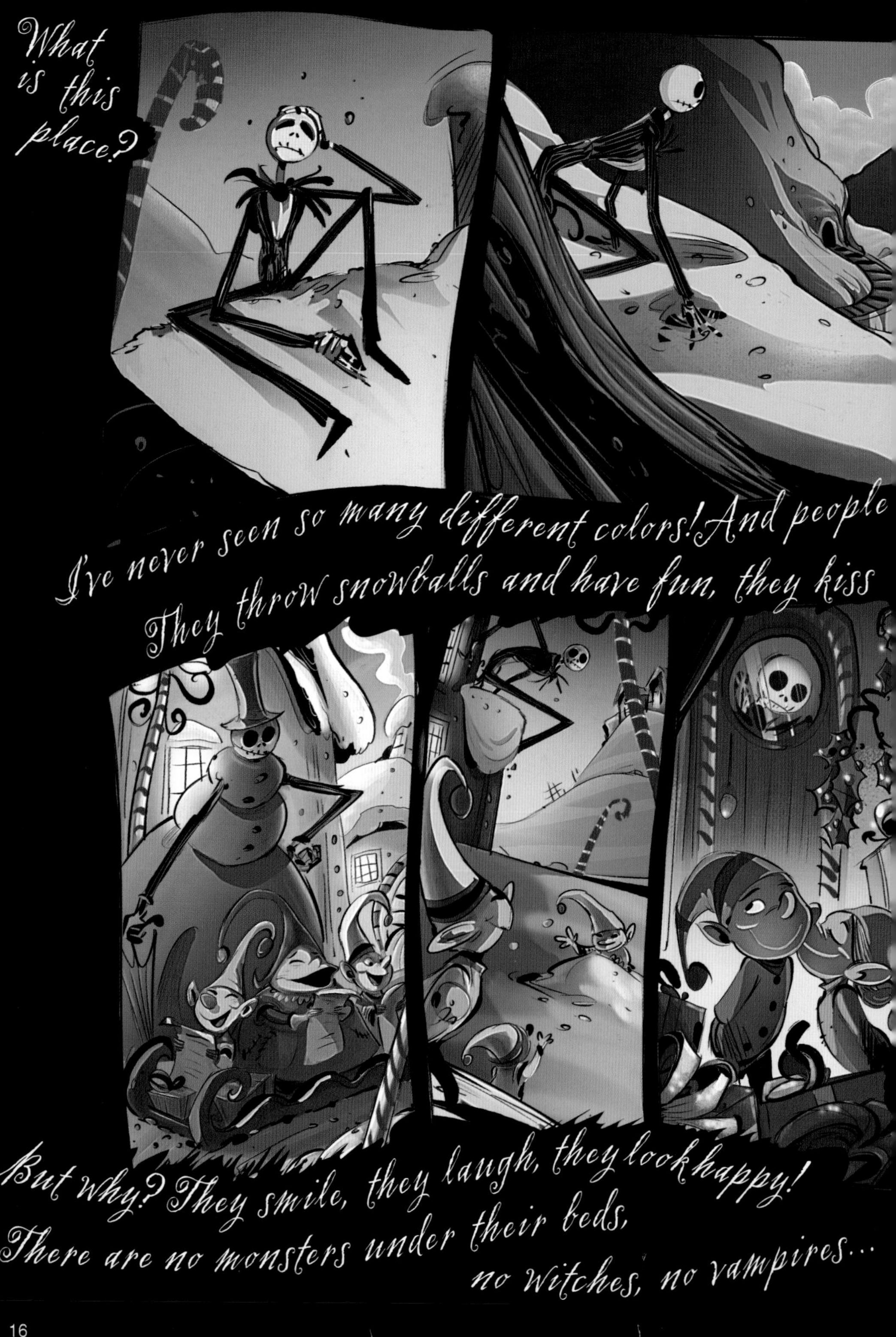
What is this place?
I've never seen so many different colors! And people
They throw snowballs and have fun, they kiss
But why? They smile, they laugh, they look happy!
There are no monsters under their beds,
no witches, no vampires...

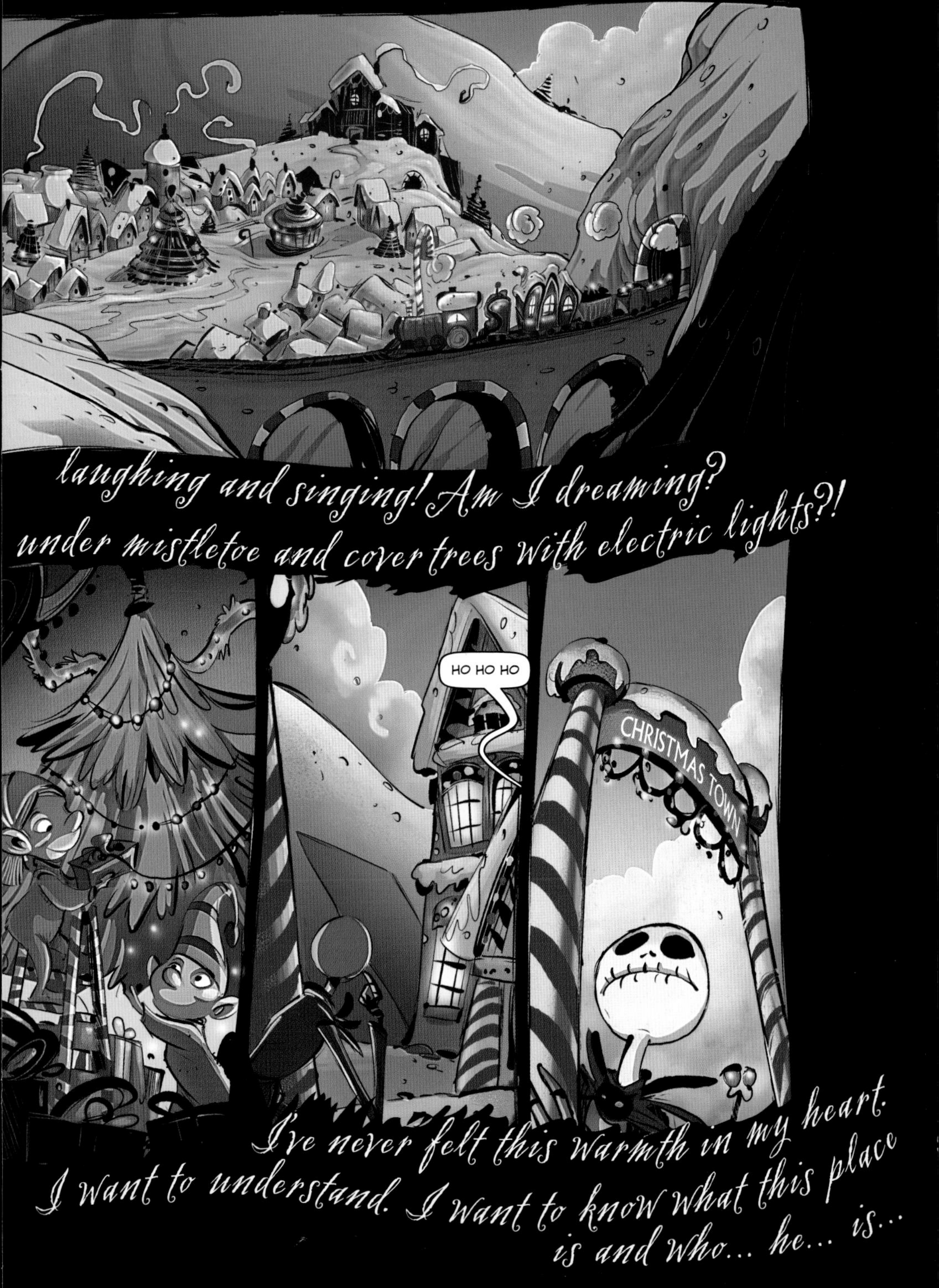
laughing and singing! Am I dreaming?
under mistletoe and cover trees with electric lights?!
HO HO HO
CHRISTMAS TOWN
I've never felt this warmth in my heart.
I want to understand. I want to know what this place
is and who... he... is...

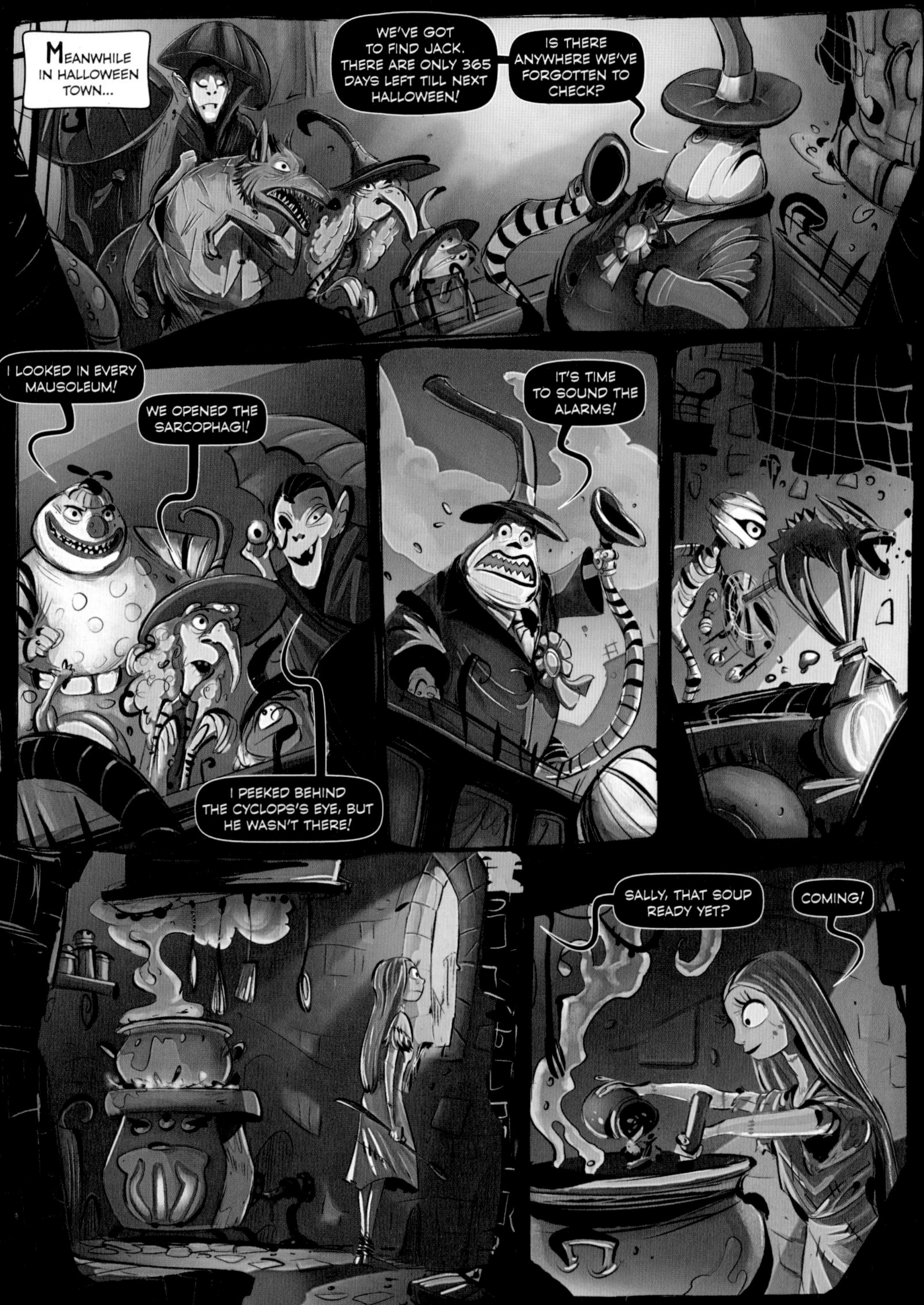

MEANWHILE IN HALLOWEEN TOWN...
WE'VE GOT TO FIND JACK. THERE ARE ONLY 365 DAYS LEFT TILL NEXT HALLOWEEN!
IS THERE ANYWHERE WE'VE FORGOTTEN TO CHECK?
I LOOKED IN EVERY MAUSOLEUM!
WE OPENED THE SARCOPHAGI!
I PEEKED BEHIND THE CYCLOPS'S EYE, BUT HE WASN'T THERE!
IT'S TIME TO SOUND THE ALARMS!
SALLY, THAT SOUP READY YET?
COMING!

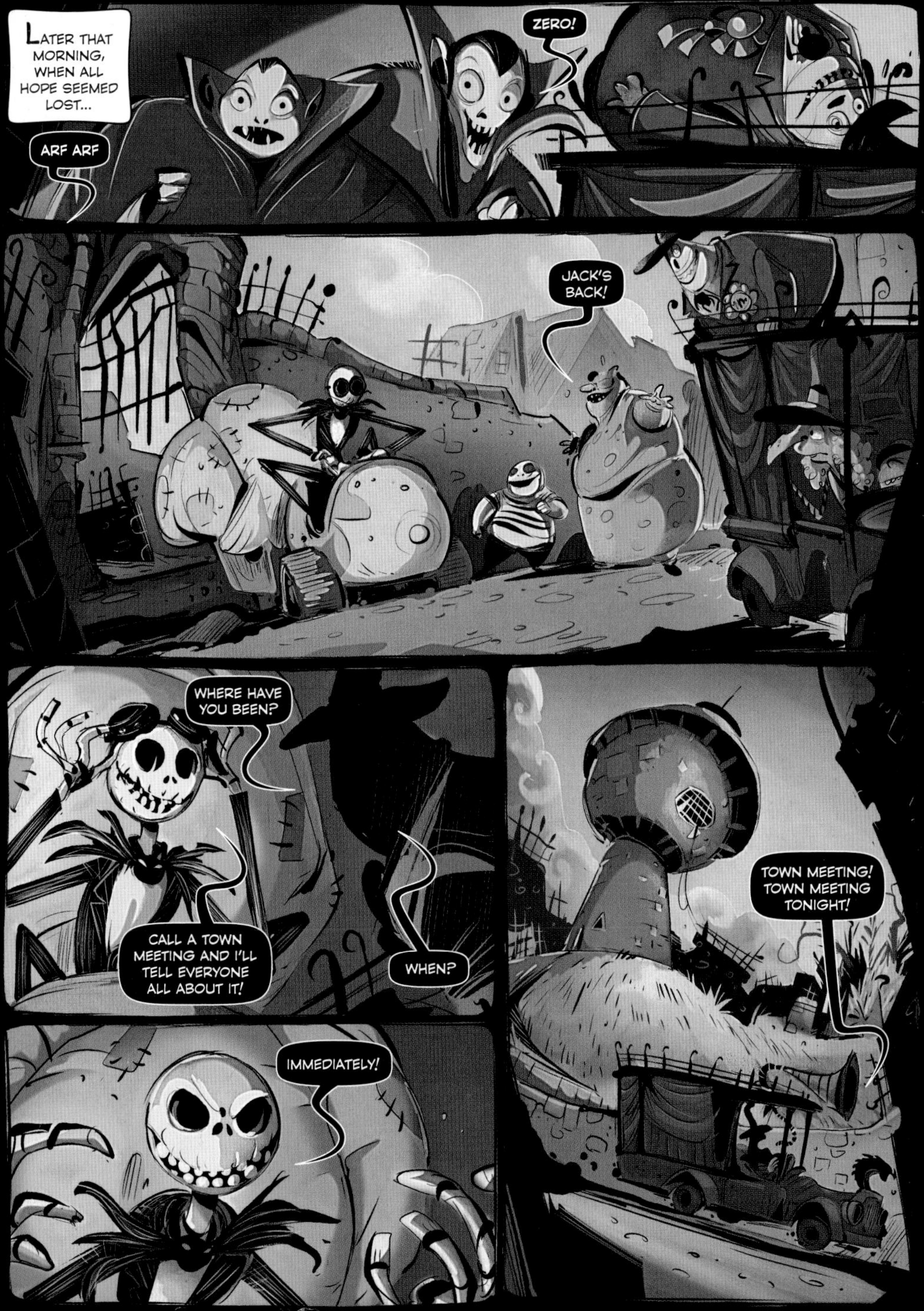
LATER THAT MORNING, WHEN ALL HOPE SEEMED LOST...
ARF ARF
ZERO!
JACK'S BACK!
WHERE HAVE YOU BEEN?
CALL A TOWN MEETING AND I'LL TELL EVERYONE ALL ABOUT IT!
WHEN?
IMMEDIATELY!
TOWN MEETING! TOWN MEETING TONIGHT!

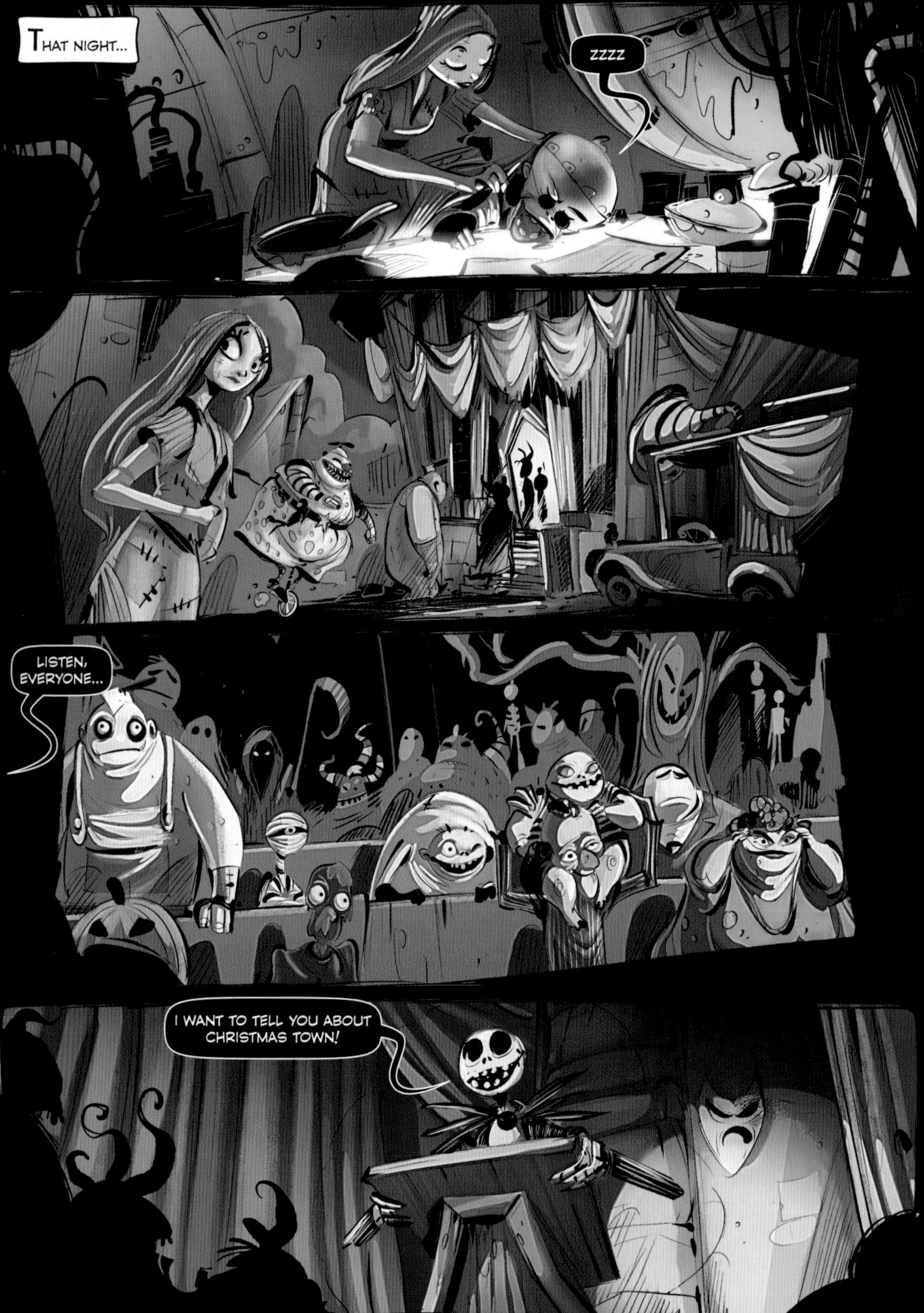
THAT NIGHT...
ZZZZ
LISTEN, EVERYONE...
I WANT TO TELL YOU ABOUT CHRISTMAS TOWN!

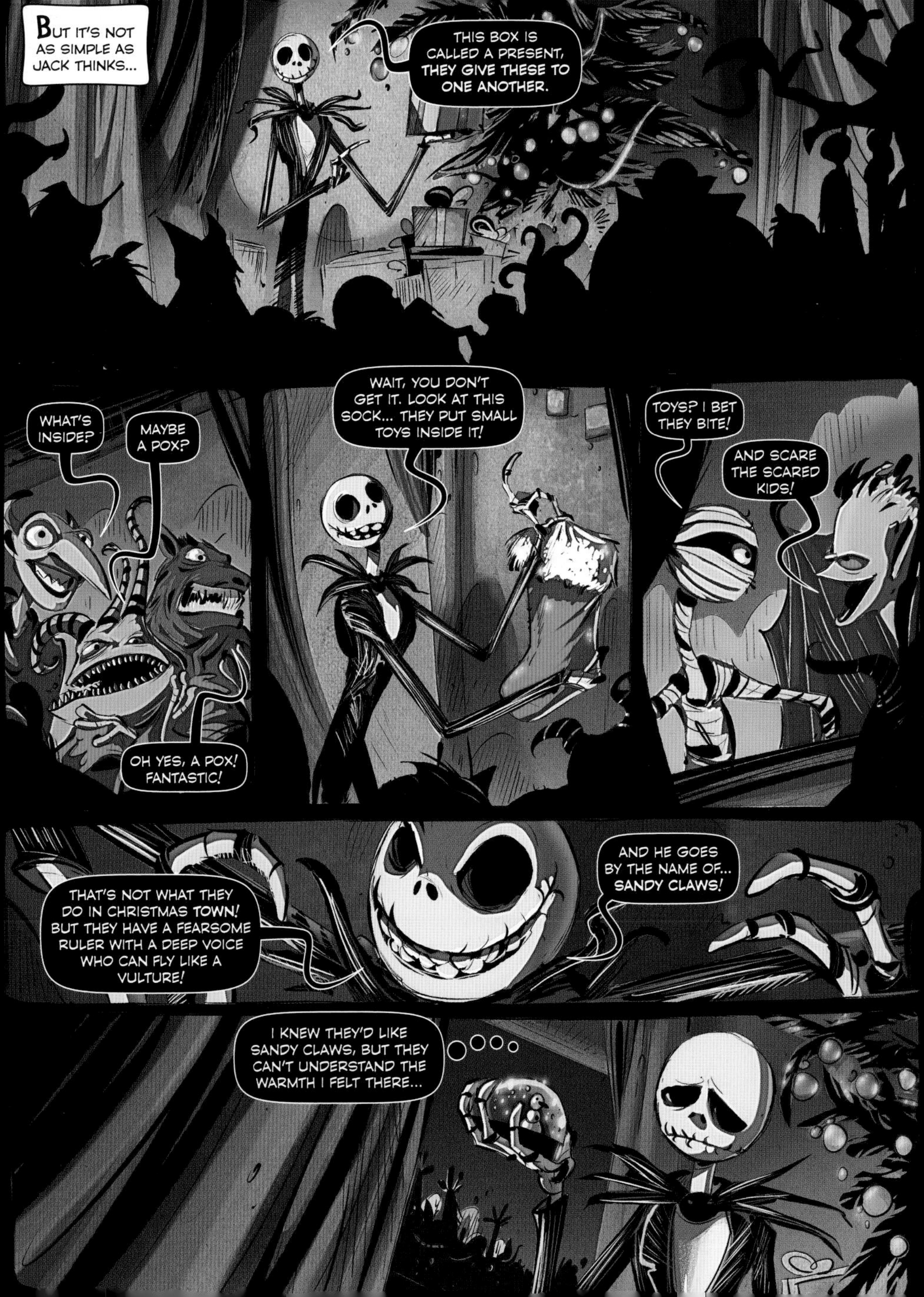

BUT IT'S NOT AS SIMPLE AS JACK THINKS...
THIS BOX IS CALLED A PRESENT, THEY GIVE THESE TO ONE ANOTHER.
WHAT'S INSIDE?
MAYBE A POX?
OH YES, A POX! FANTASTIC!
WAIT, YOU DON'T GET IT. LOOK AT THIS SOCK... THEY PUT SMALL TOYS INSIDE IT!
TOYS? I BET THEY BITE!
AND SCARE THE SCARED KIDS!
THAT'S NOT WHAT THEY DO IN CHRISTMAS TOWN! BUT THEY HAVE A FEARSOME RULER WITH A DEEP VOICE WHO CAN FLY LIKE A VULTURE!
AND HE GOES BY THE NAME OF... SANDY CLAWS!
I KNEW THEY'D LIKE SANDY CLAWS, BUT THEY CAN'T UNDERSTAND THE WARMTH I FELT THERE...

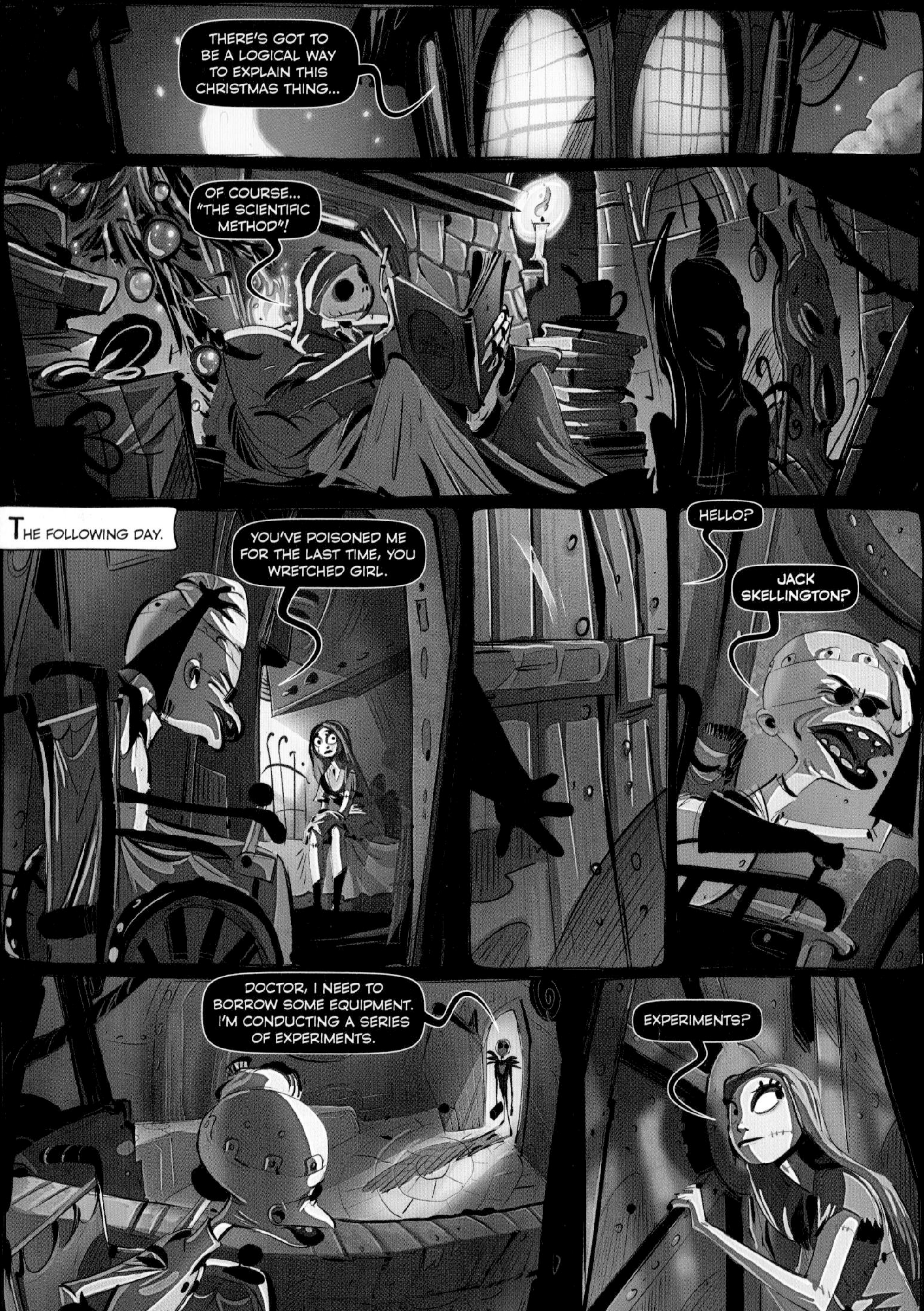
THERE'S GOT TO BE A LOGICAL WAY TO EXPLAIN THIS CHRISTMAS THING...
OF COURSE... "THE SCIENTIFIC METHOD"!
THE FOLLOWING DAY.
YOU'VE POISONED ME FOR THE LAST TIME, YOU WRETCHED GIRL.
HELLO?
JACK SKELLINGTON?
DOCTOR, I NEED TO BORROW SOME EQUIPMENT. I'M CONDUCTING A SERIES OF EXPERIMENTS.
EXPERIMENTS?

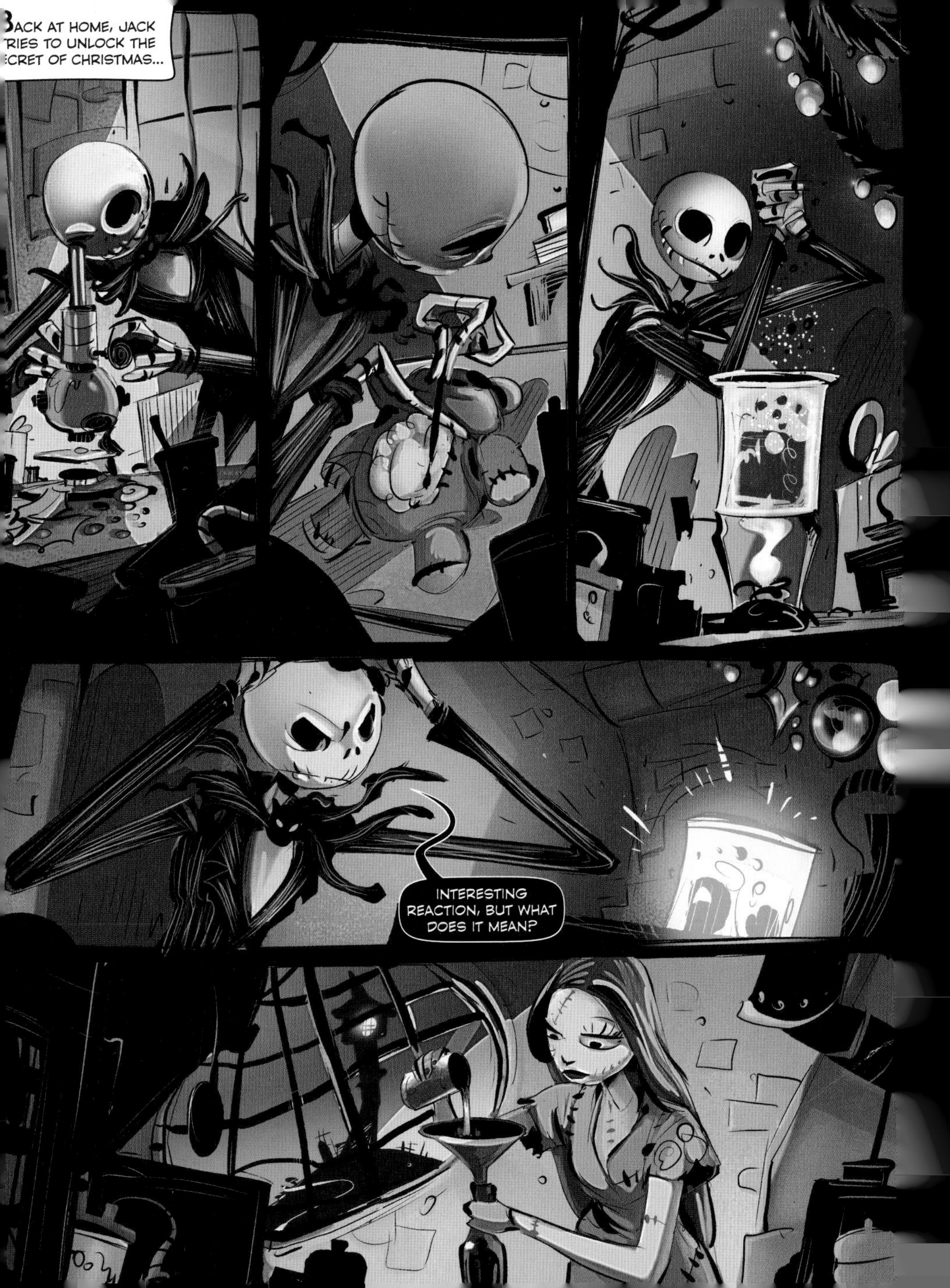
BACK AT HOME, JACK TRIES TO UNLOCK THE SECRET OF CHRISTMAS...
INTERESTING REACTION, BUT WHAT DOES IT MEAN?

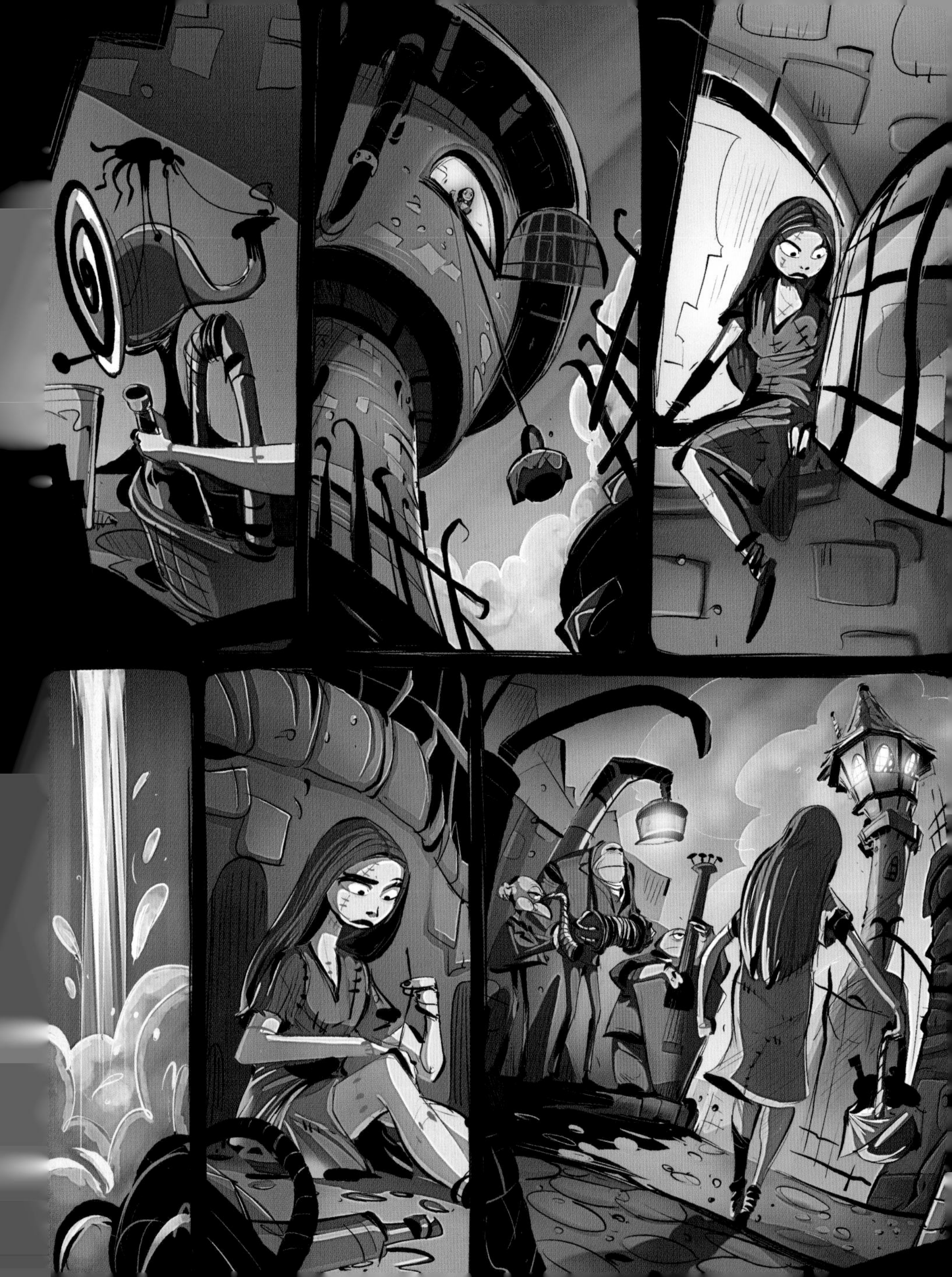

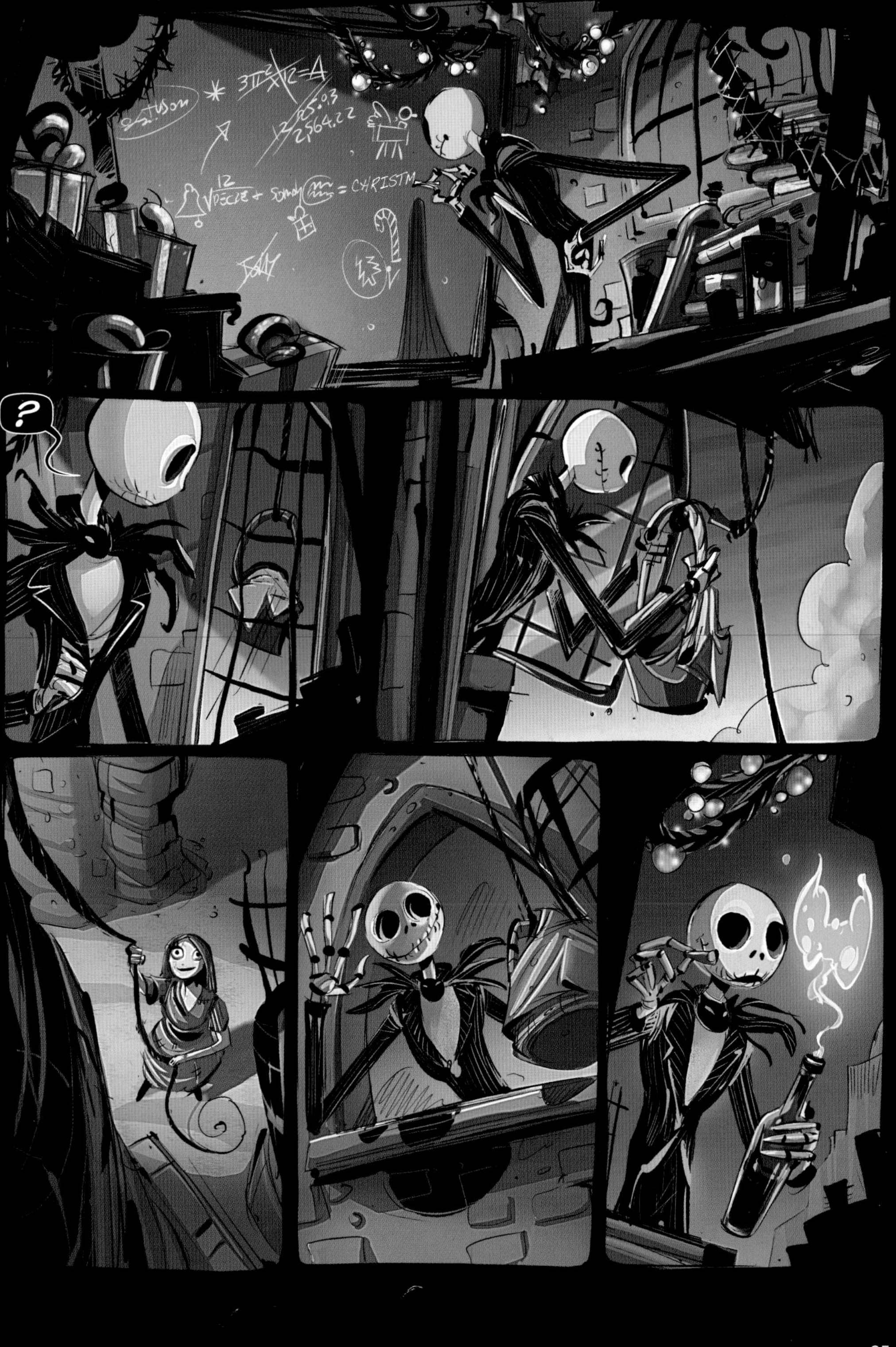
= CHRISTM
?

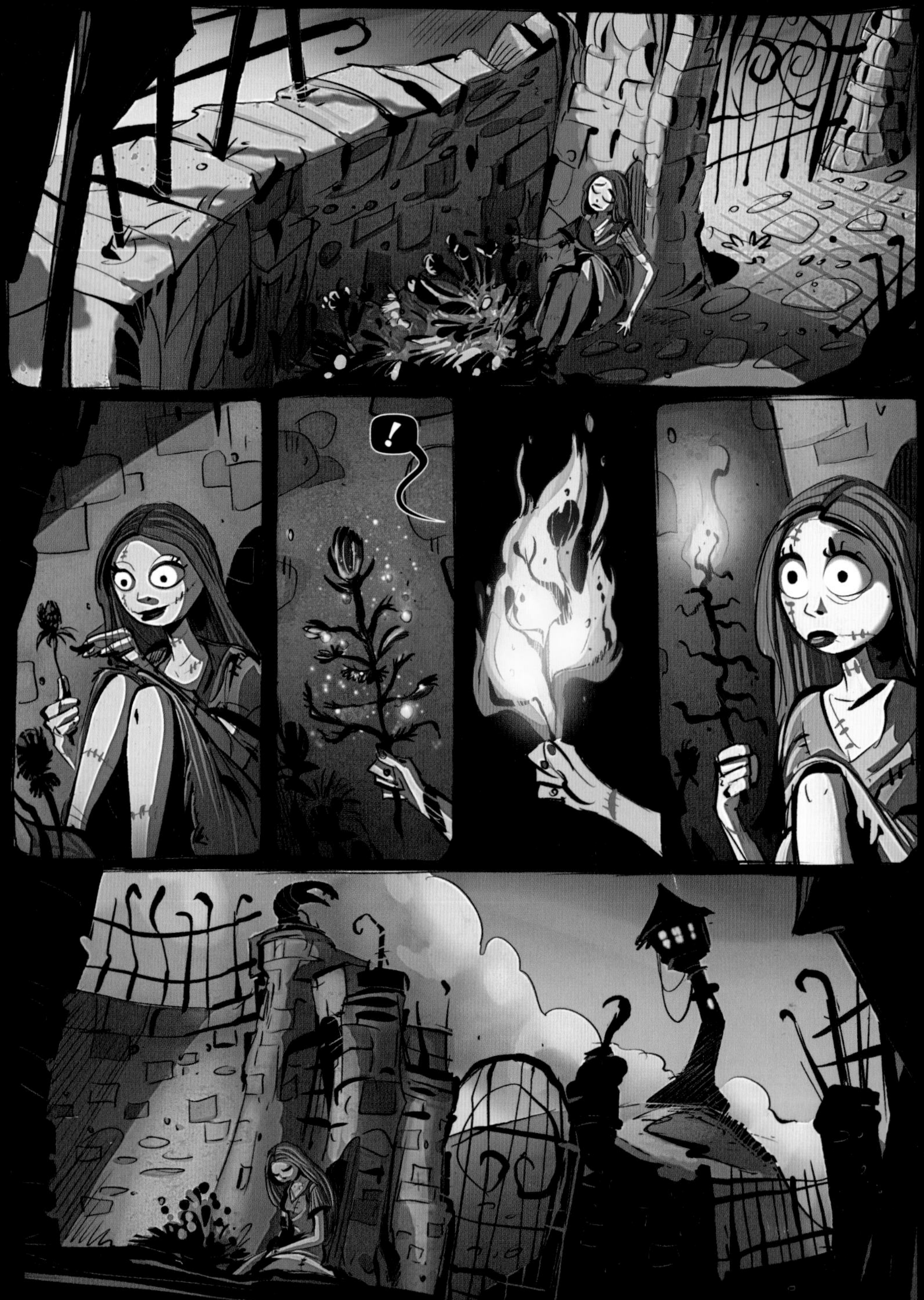
!

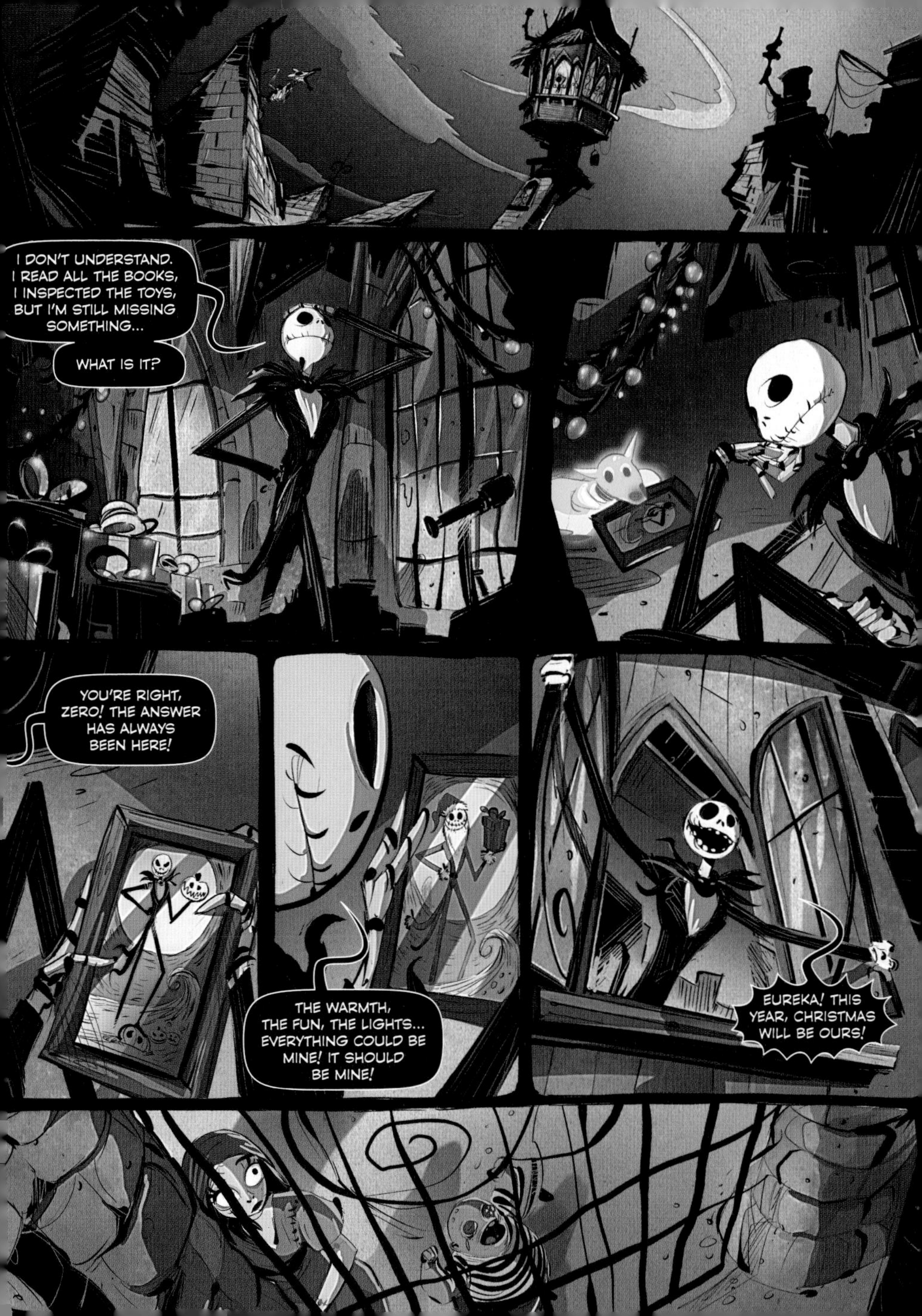
I DON'T UNDERSTAND. I READ ALL THE BOOKS, I INSPECTED THE TOYS, BUT I'M STILL MISSING SOMETHING...
WHAT IS IT?
YOU'RE RIGHT, ZERO! THE ANSWER HAS ALWAYS BEEN HERE!
THE WARMTH, THE FUN, THE LIGHTS... EVERYTHING COULD BE MINE! IT SHOULD BE MINE!
EUREKA! THIS YEAR, CHRISTMAS WILL BE OURS!

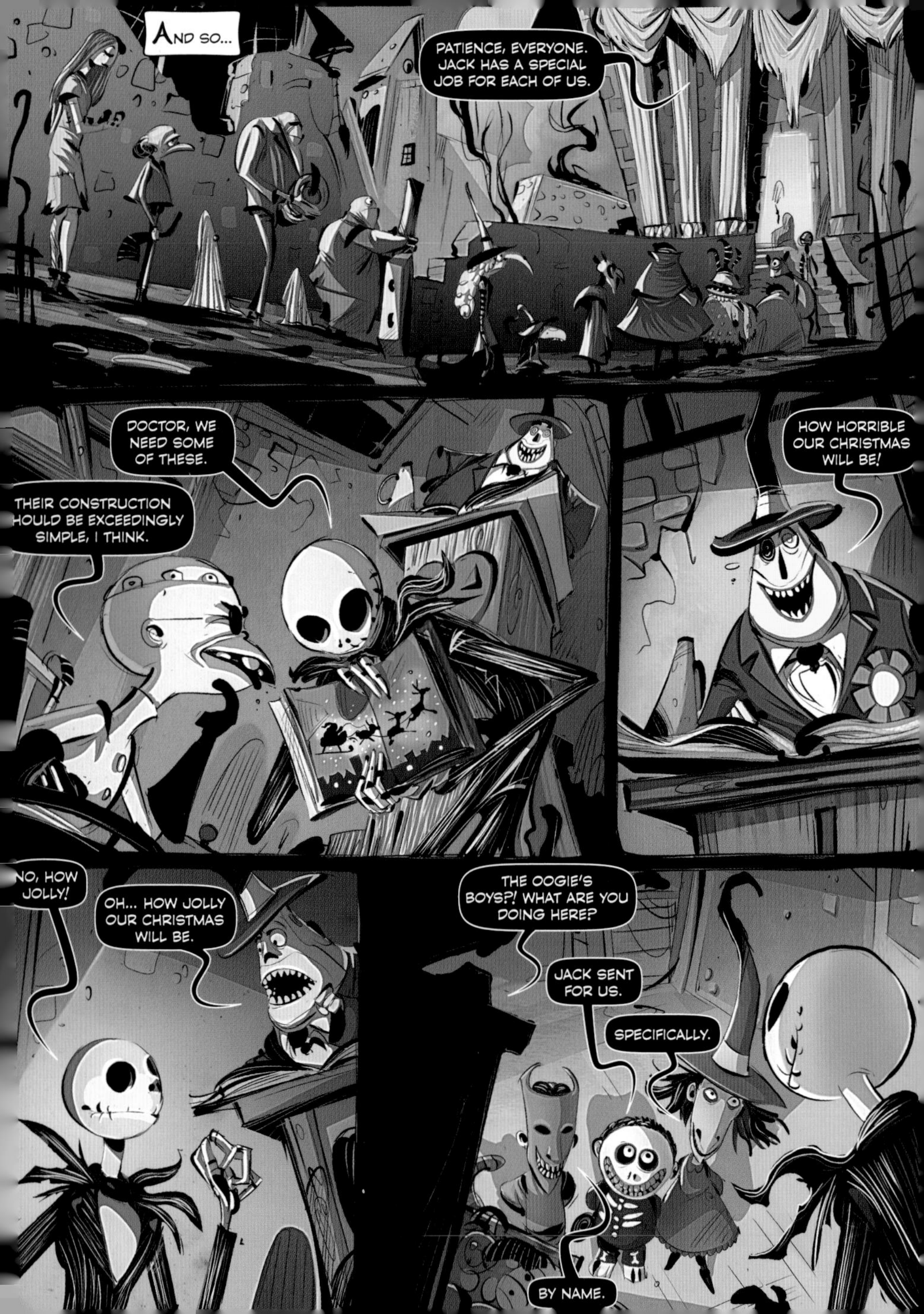
AND SO...
PATIENCE, EVERYONE. JACK HAS A SPECIAL JOB FOR EACH OF US.
DOCTOR, WE NEED SOME OF THESE.
THEIR CONSTRUCTION HOULD BE EXCEEDINGLY SIMPLE, I THINK.
HOW HORRIBLE OUR CHRISTMAS WILL BE!
NO, HOW JOLLY!
OH... HOW JOLLY OUR CHRISTMAS WILL BE.
THE OOGIE'S BOYS?! WHAT ARE YOU DOING HERE?
JACK SENT FOR US.
SPECIFICALLY.
BY NAME.

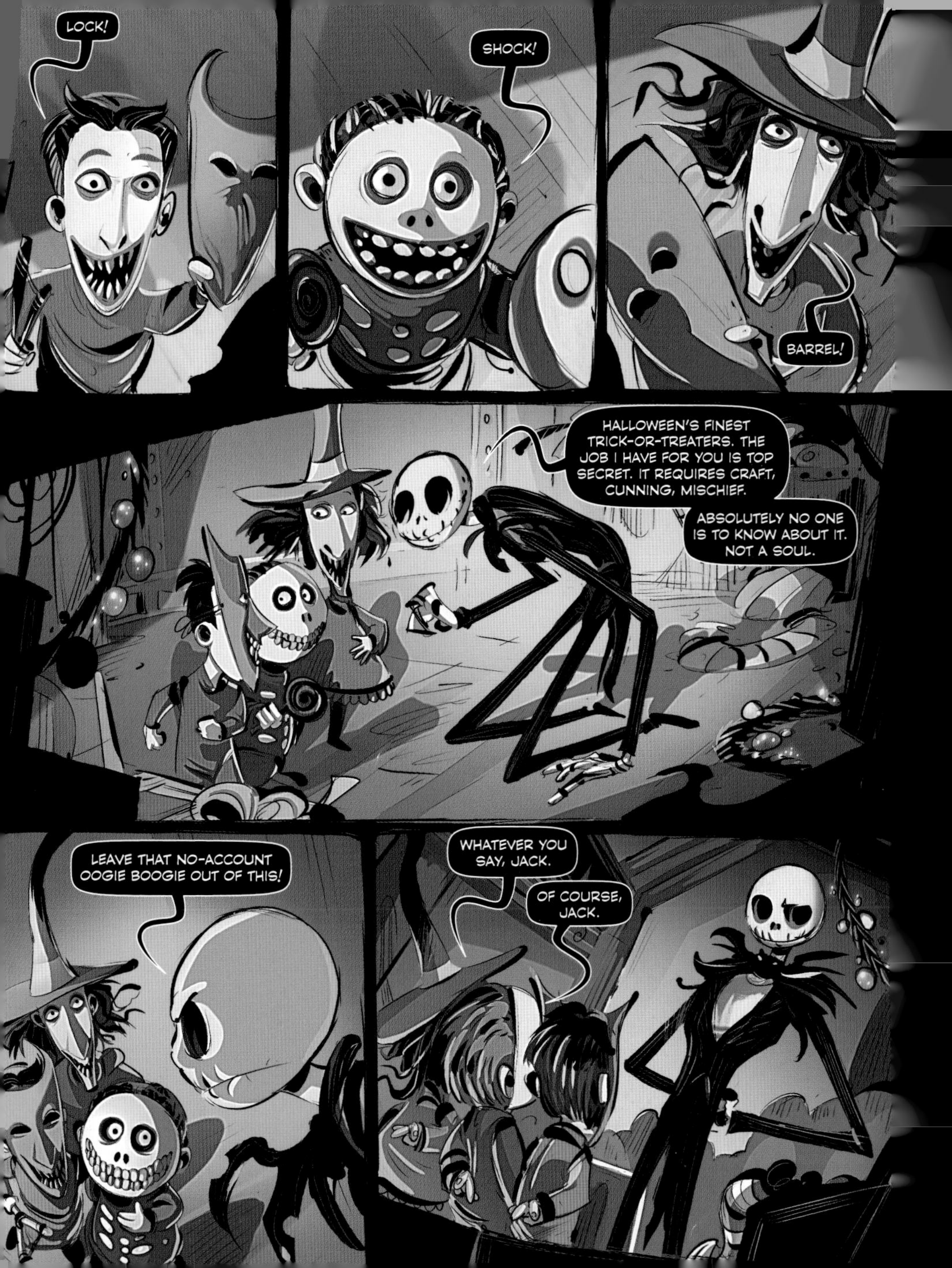
LOCK!
SHOCK!
BARREL!
HALLOWEEN'S FINEST TRICK-OR-TREATERS. THE JOB I HAVE FOR YOU IS TOP SECRET. IT REQUIRES CRAFT, CUNNING, MISCHIEF.
ABSOLUTELY NO ONE IS TO KNOW ABOUT IT. NOT A SOUL.
LEAVE THAT NO-ACCOUNT OOGIE BOOGIE OUT OF THIS!
WHATEVER YOU SAY, JACK.
OF COURSE, JACK.

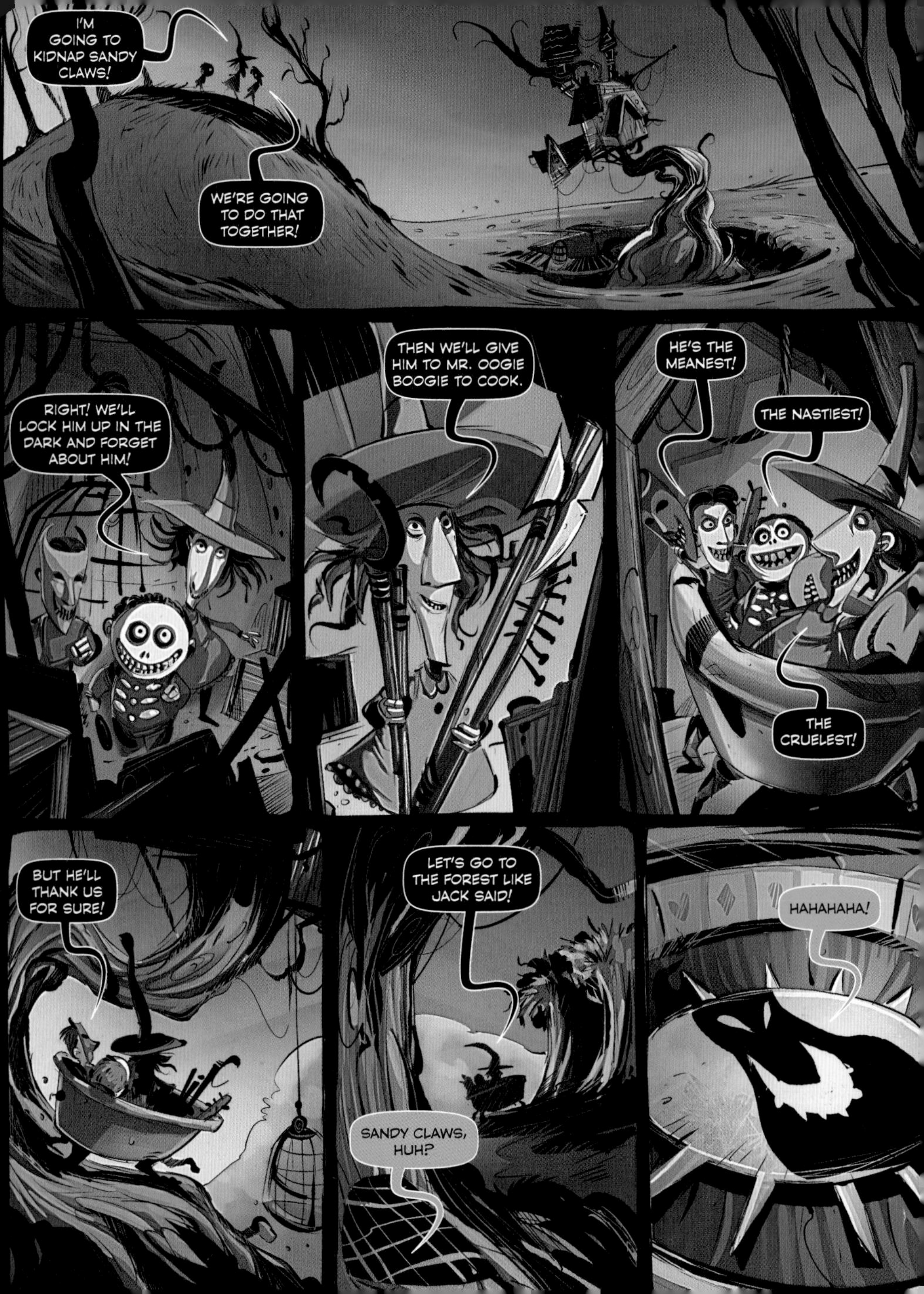
I'M GOING TO KIDNAP SANDY CLAWS!
WE'RE GOING TO DO THAT TOGETHER!
RIGHT! WE'LL LOCK HIM UP IN THE DARK AND FORGET ABOUT HIM!
THEN WE'LL GIVE HIM TO MR. OOGIE BOOGIE TO COOK.
HE'S THE MEANEST!
THE NASTIEST!
THE CRUELEST!
BUT HE'LL THANK US FOR SURE!
LET'S GO TO THE FOREST LIKE JACK SAID!
SANDY CLAWS, HUH?
HAHAHAHA!

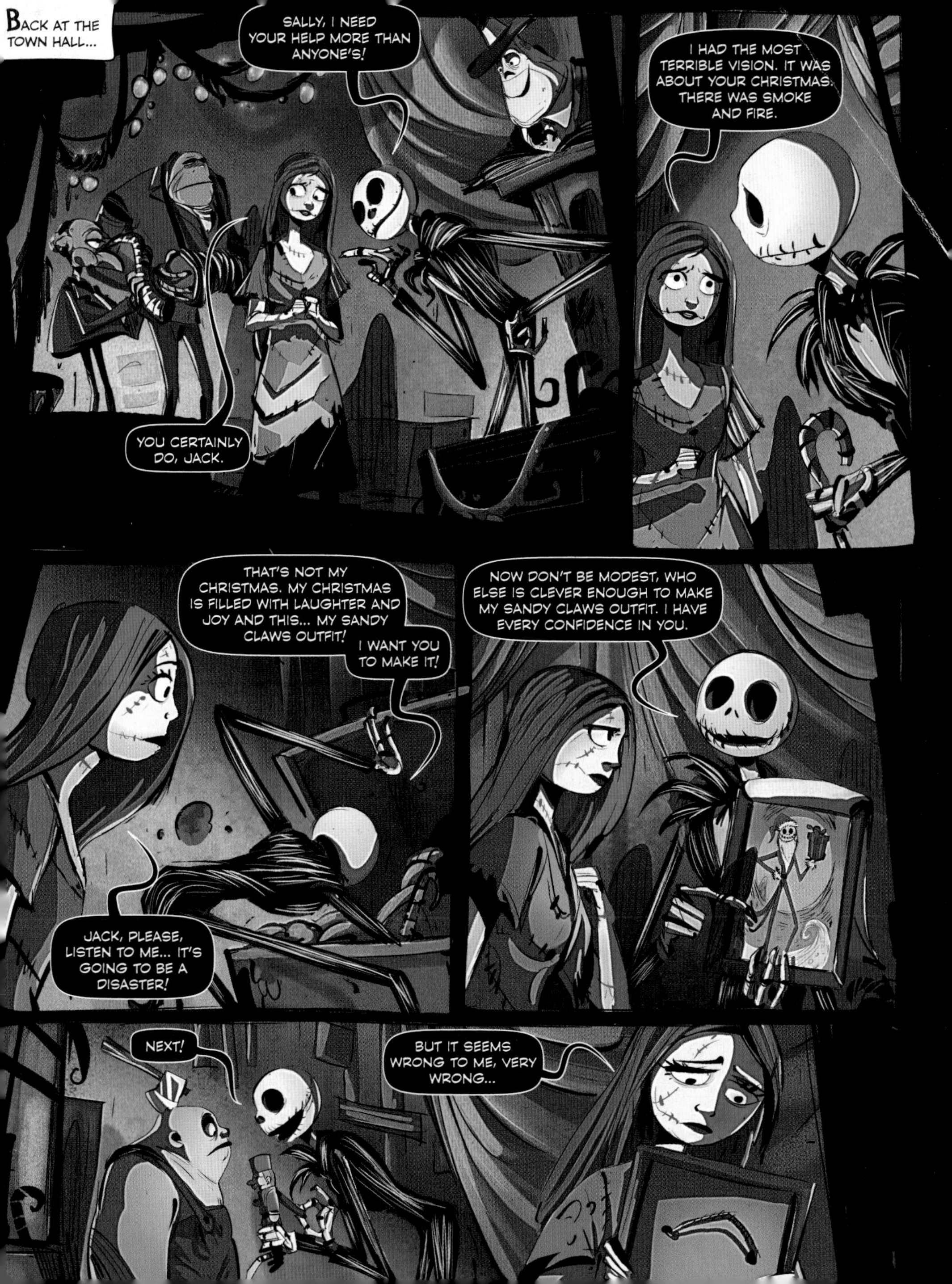
BACK AT THE TOWN HALL...
SALLY, I NEED YOUR HELP MORE THAN ANYONE'S!
YOU CERTAINLY DO, JACK.
I HAD THE MOST TERRIBLE VISION. IT WAS ABOUT YOUR CHRISTMAS. THERE WAS SMOKE AND FIRE.
THAT'S NOT MY CHRISTMAS. MY CHRISTMAS IS FILLED WITH LAUGHTER AND JOY AND THIS... MY SANDY CLAWS OUTFIT!
I WANT YOU TO MAKE IT!
JACK, PLEASE, LISTEN TO ME... IT'S GOING TO BE A DISASTER!
NOW DON'T BE MODEST, WHO ELSE IS CLEVER ENOUGH TO MAKE MY SANDY CLAWS OUTFIT. I HAVE EVERY CONFIDENCE IN YOU.
NEXT!
BUT IT SEEMS WRONG TO ME, VERY WRONG...

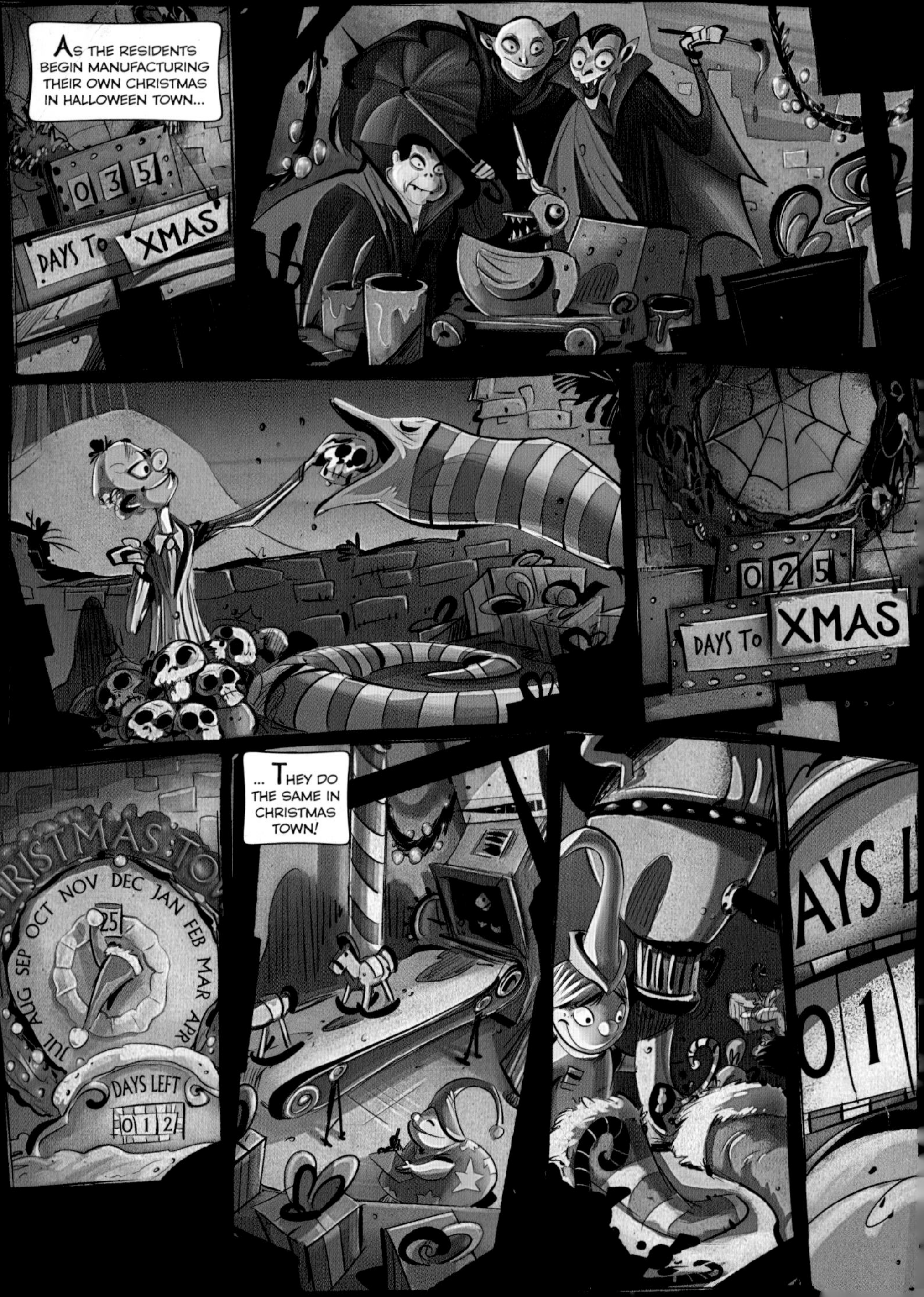
AS THE RESIDENTS BEGIN MANUFACTURING THEIR OWN CHRISTMAS IN HALLOWEEN TOWN...
035
DAYS TO XMAS
025
DAYS TO XMAS
... THEY DO THE SAME IN CHRISTMAS TOWN!
JUL AUG SEP OCT NOV DEC JAN FEB MAR APR
25
DAYS LEFT
012

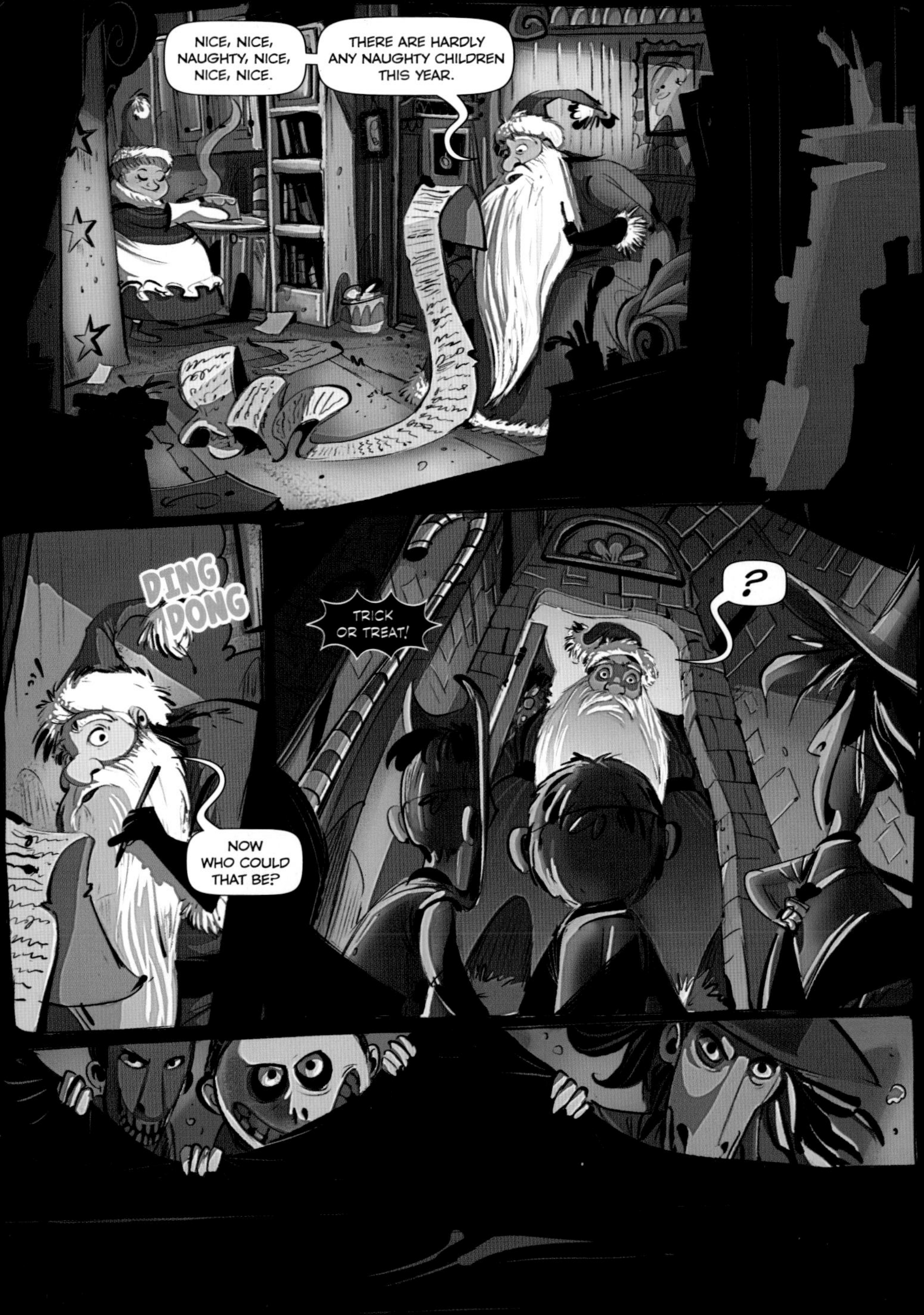
NICE, NICE, NAUGHTY, NICE, NICE, NICE.
THERE ARE HARDLY ANY NAUGHTY CHILDREN THIS YEAR.
DING DONG
NOW WHO COULD THAT BE?
TRICK OR TREAT!
?

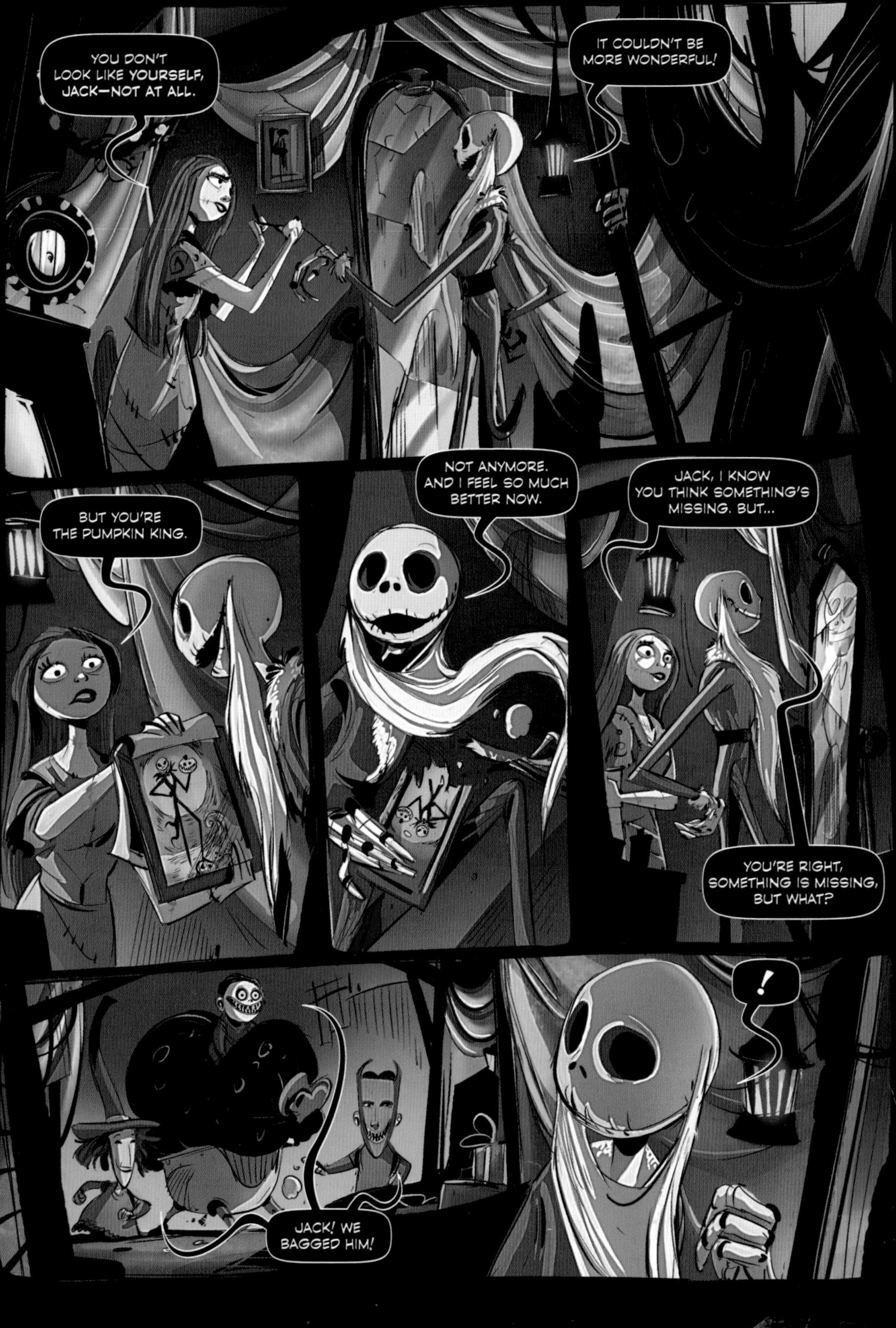
YOU DON'T LOOK LIKE YOURSELF, JACK—NOT AT ALL.
IT COULDN'T BE MORE WONDERFUL!
BUT YOU'RE THE PUMPKIN KING.
NOT ANYMORE. AND I FEEL SO MUCH BETTER NOW.
JACK, I KNOW YOU THINK SOMETHING'S MISSING. BUT...
YOU'RE RIGHT, SOMETHING IS MISSING, BUT WHAT?
JACK! WE BAGGED HIM!
!

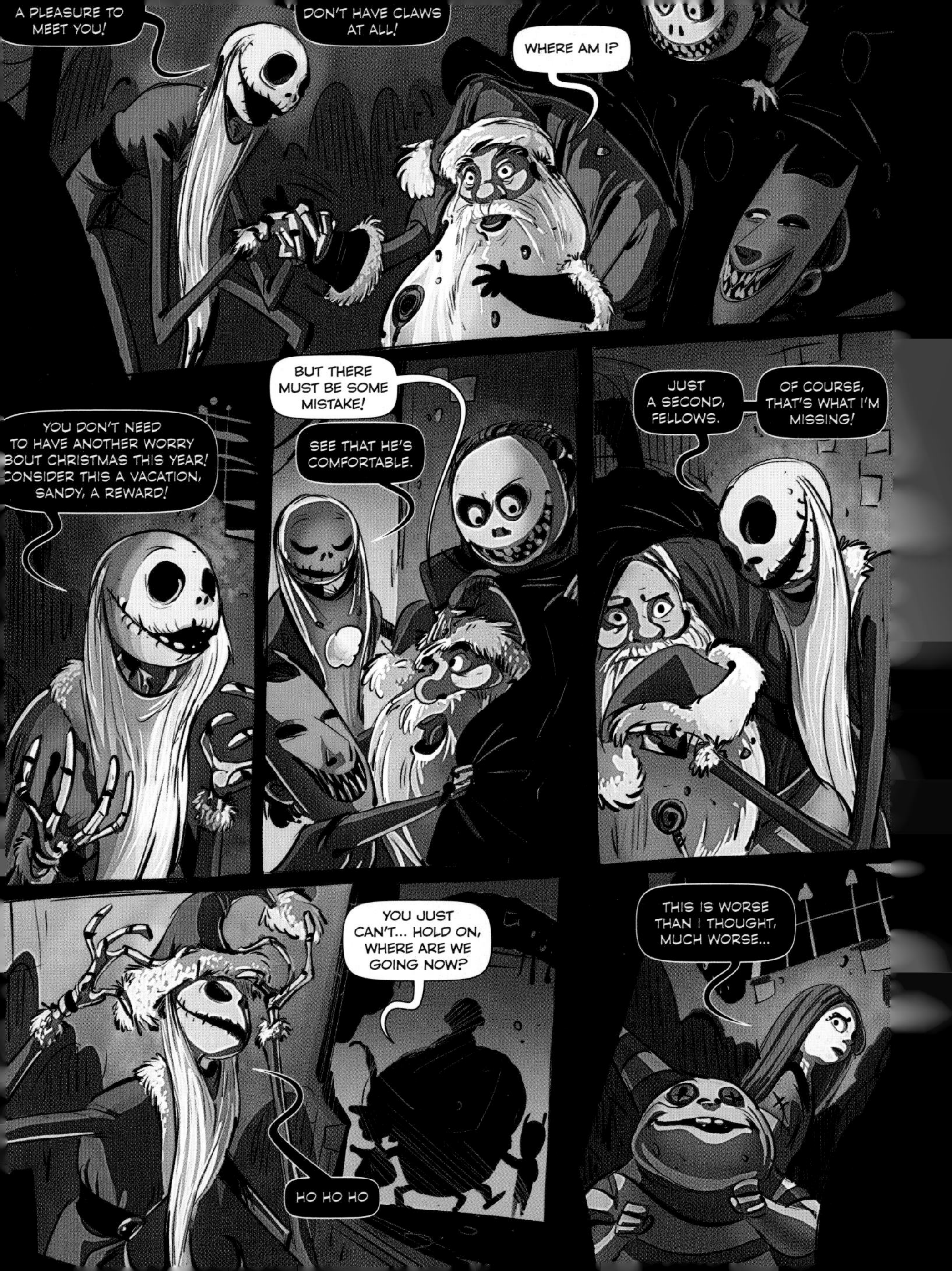
A PLEASURE TO MEET YOU!
DON'T HAVE CLAWS AT ALL!
WHERE AM I?
YOU DON'T NEED TO HAVE ANOTHER WORRY BOUT CHRISTMAS THIS YEAR! CONSIDER THIS A VACATION, SANDY, A REWARD!
BUT THERE MUST BE SOME MISTAKE!
SEE THAT HE'S COMFORTABLE.
JUST A SECOND, FELLOWS.
OF COURSE, THAT'S WHAT I'M MISSING!
YOU JUST CAN'T... HOLD ON, WHERE ARE WE GOING NOW?
HO HO HO
THIS IS WORSE THAN I THOUGHT, MUCH WORSE...

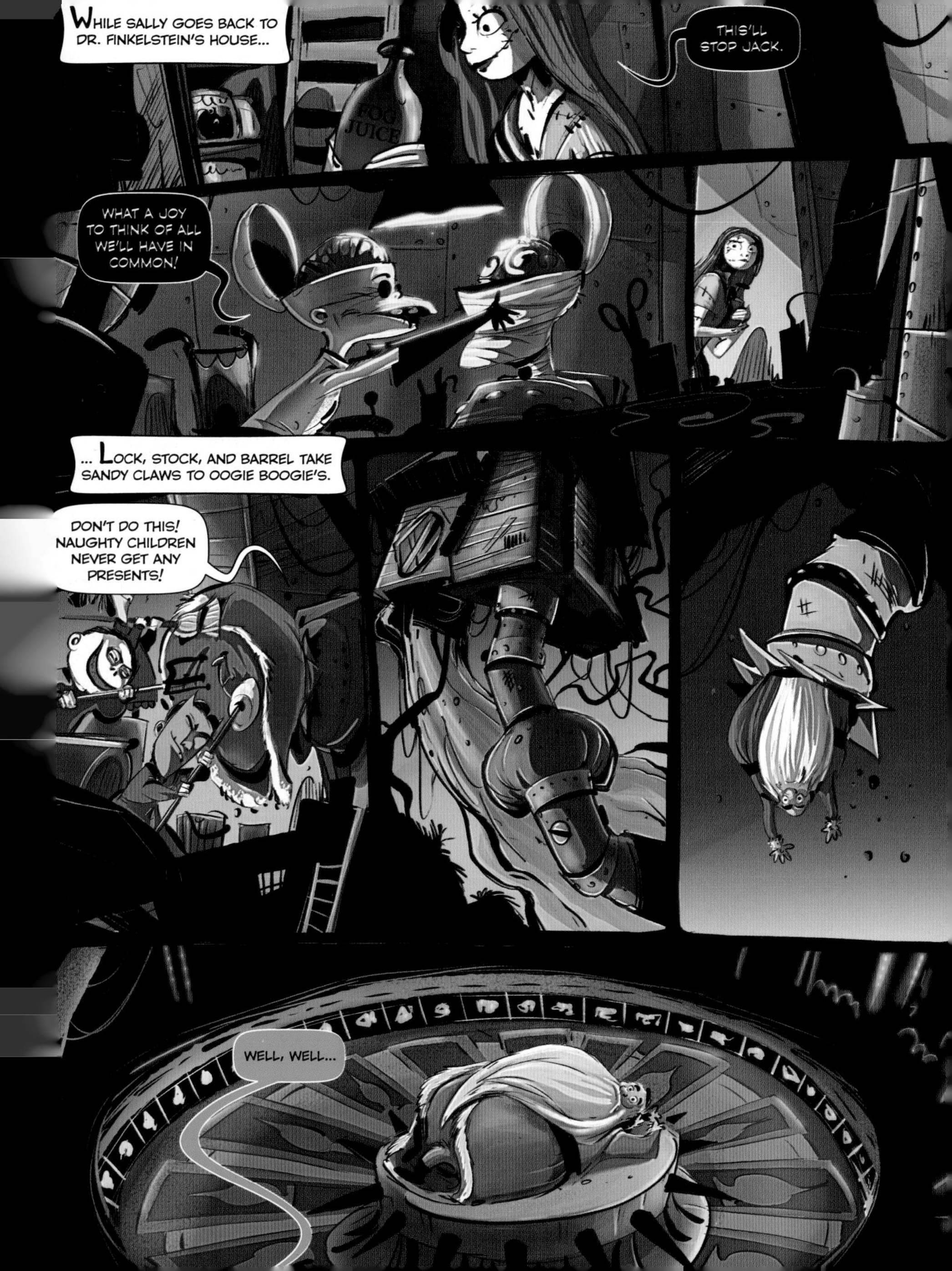
WHILE SALLY GOES BACK TO DR. FINKELSTEIN'S HOUSE...
THIS'LL STOP JACK.
FOG JUICE
WHAT A JOY TO THINK OF ALL WE'LL HAVE IN COMMON!
... LOCK, STOCK, AND BARREL TAKE SANDY CLAWS TO OOGIE BOOGIE'S.
DON'T DO THIS! NAUGHTY CHILDREN NEVER GET ANY PRESENTS!
WELL, WELL...

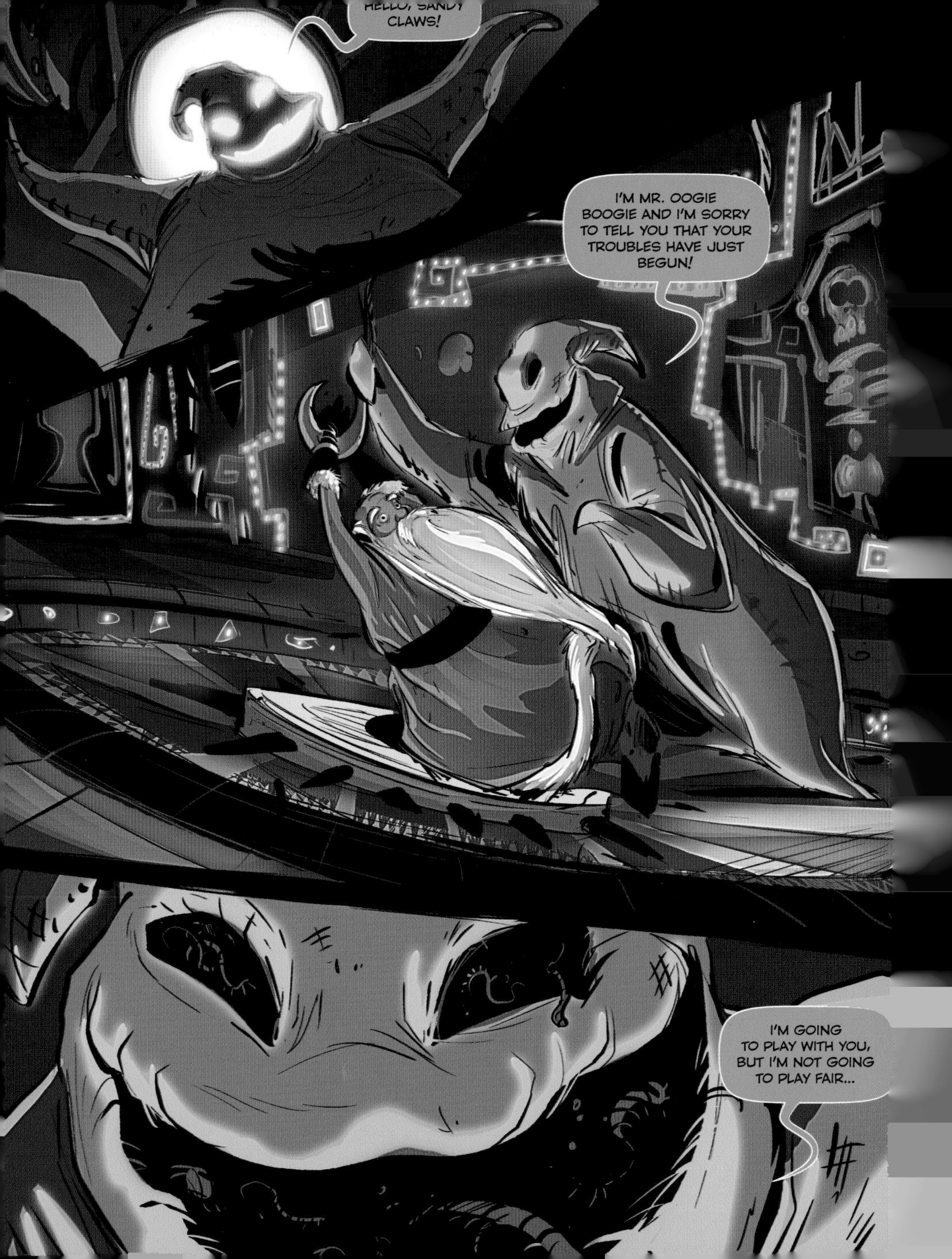
HELLO, SANDY CLAWS!
I'M MR. OOGIE BOOGIE AND I'M SORRY TO TELL YOU THAT YOUR TROUBLES HAVE JUST BEGUN!
I'M GOING TO PLAY WITH YOU, BUT I'M NOT GOING TO PLAY FAIR...

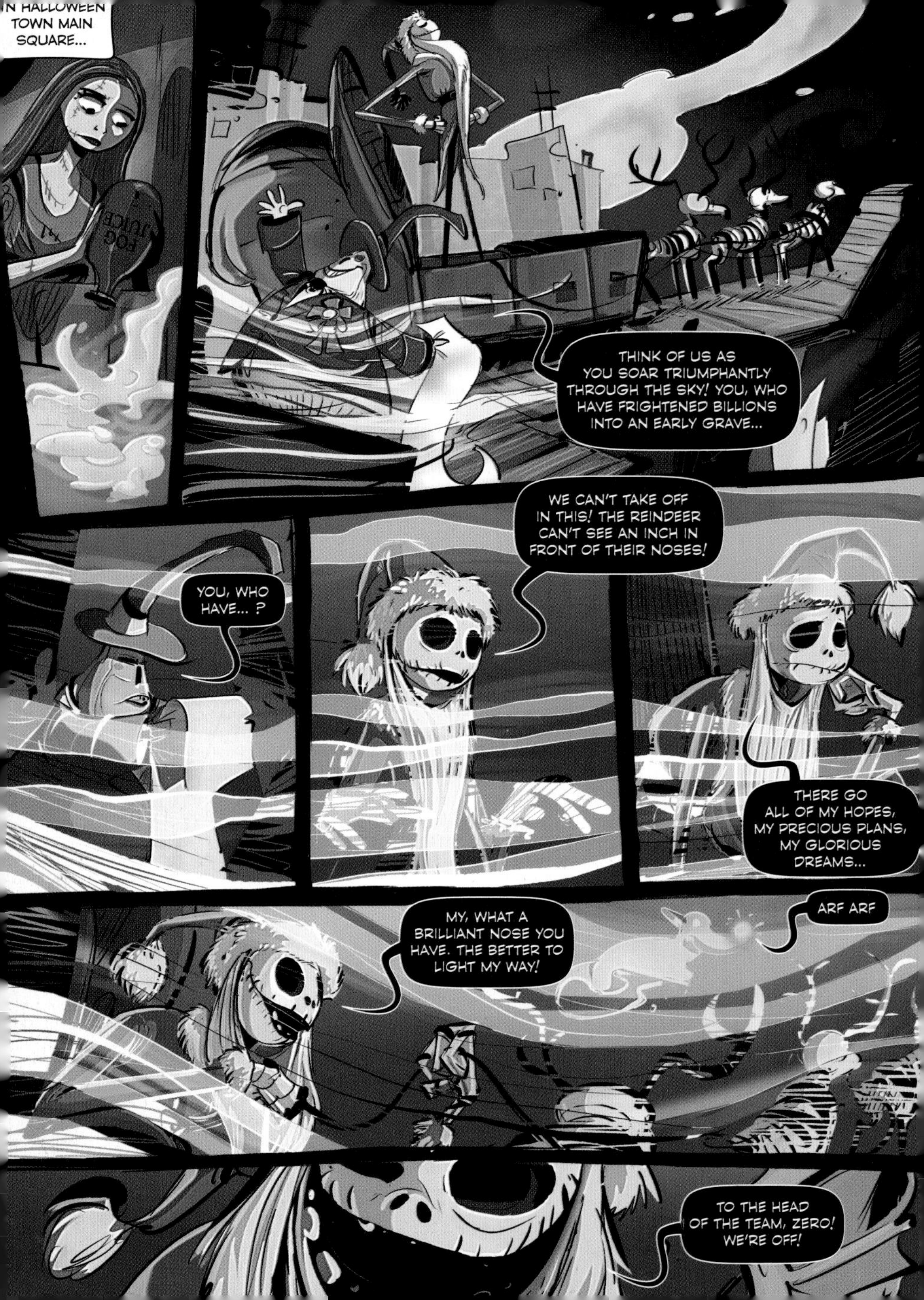
N HALLOWEEN TOWN MAIN SQUARE...
JUICE FOG
THINK OF US AS YOU SOAR TRIUMPHANTLY THROUGH THE SKY! YOU, WHO HAVE FRIGHTENED BILLIONS INTO AN EARLY GRAVE...
YOU, WHO HAVE... ?
WE CAN'T TAKE OFF IN THIS! THE REINDEER CAN'T SEE AN INCH IN FRONT OF THEIR NOSES!
THERE GO ALL OF MY HOPES, MY PRECIOUS PLANS, MY GLORIOUS DREAMS...
MY, WHAT A BRILLIANT NOSE YOU HAVE. THE BETTER TO LIGHT MY WAY!
ARF ARF
TO THE HEAD OF THE TEAM, ZERO! WE'RE OFF!

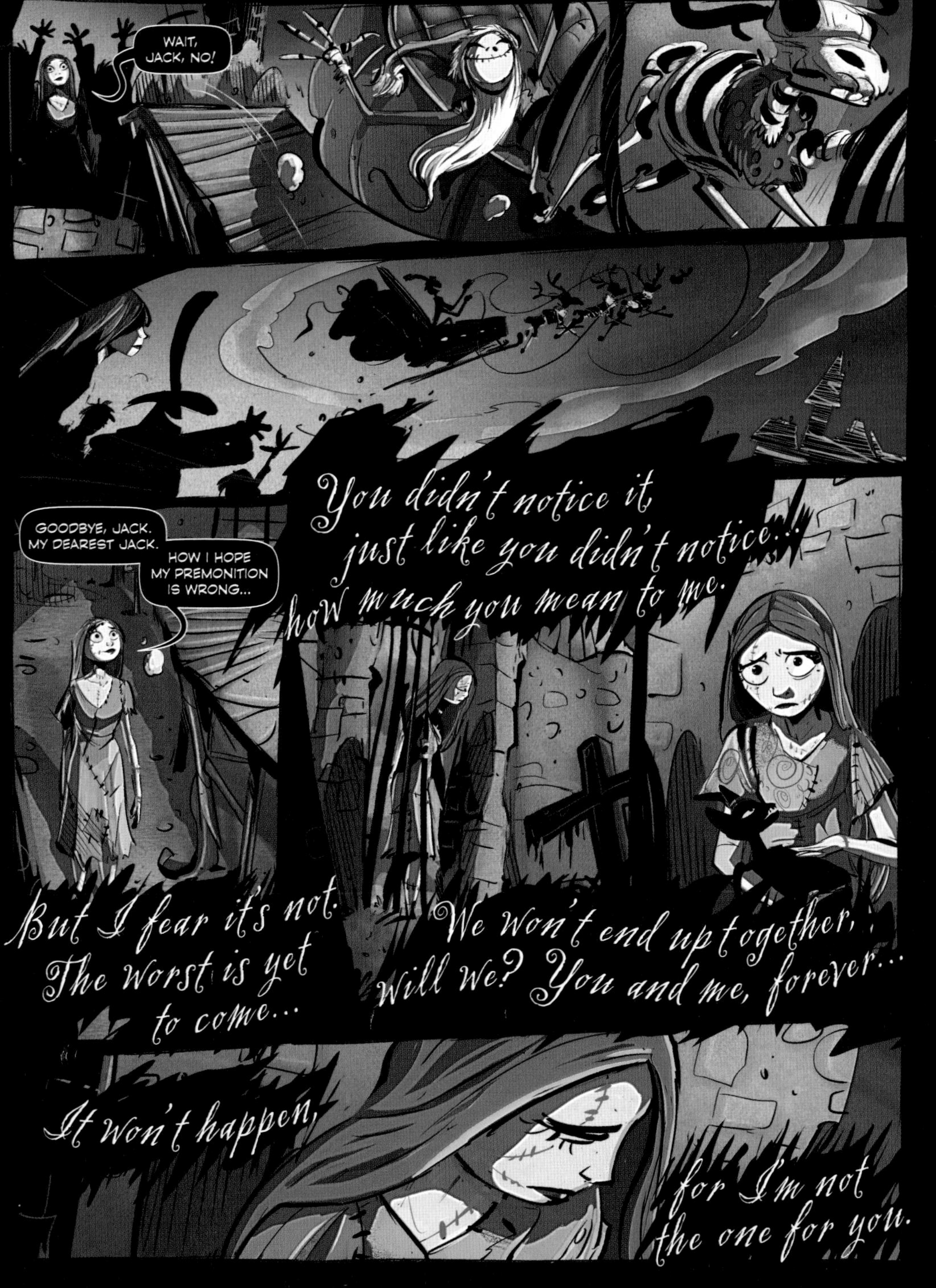
WAIT, JACK, NO!
You didn't notice it just like you didn't notice... how much you mean to me.
GOODBYE, JACK. MY DEAREST JACK.
HOW I HOPE MY PREMONITION IS WRONG...
But I fear it's not. The worst is yet to come...
We won't end up together, will we? You and me, forever...
It won't happen,
for I'm not the one for you.

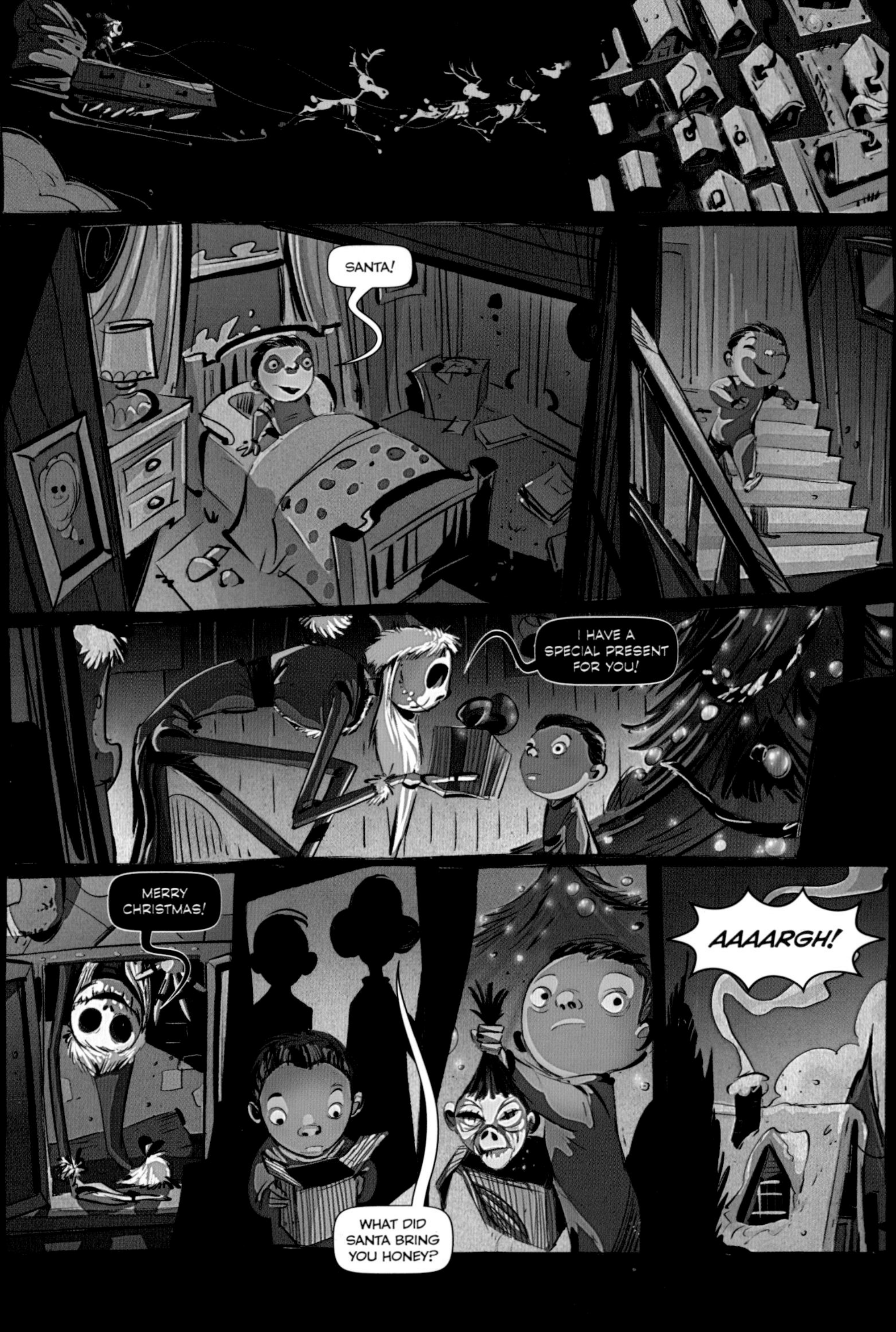
SANTA!
I HAVE A SPECIAL PRESENT FOR YOU!
MERRY CHRISTMAS!
WHAT DID SANTA BRING YOU HONEY?
AAAARGH!

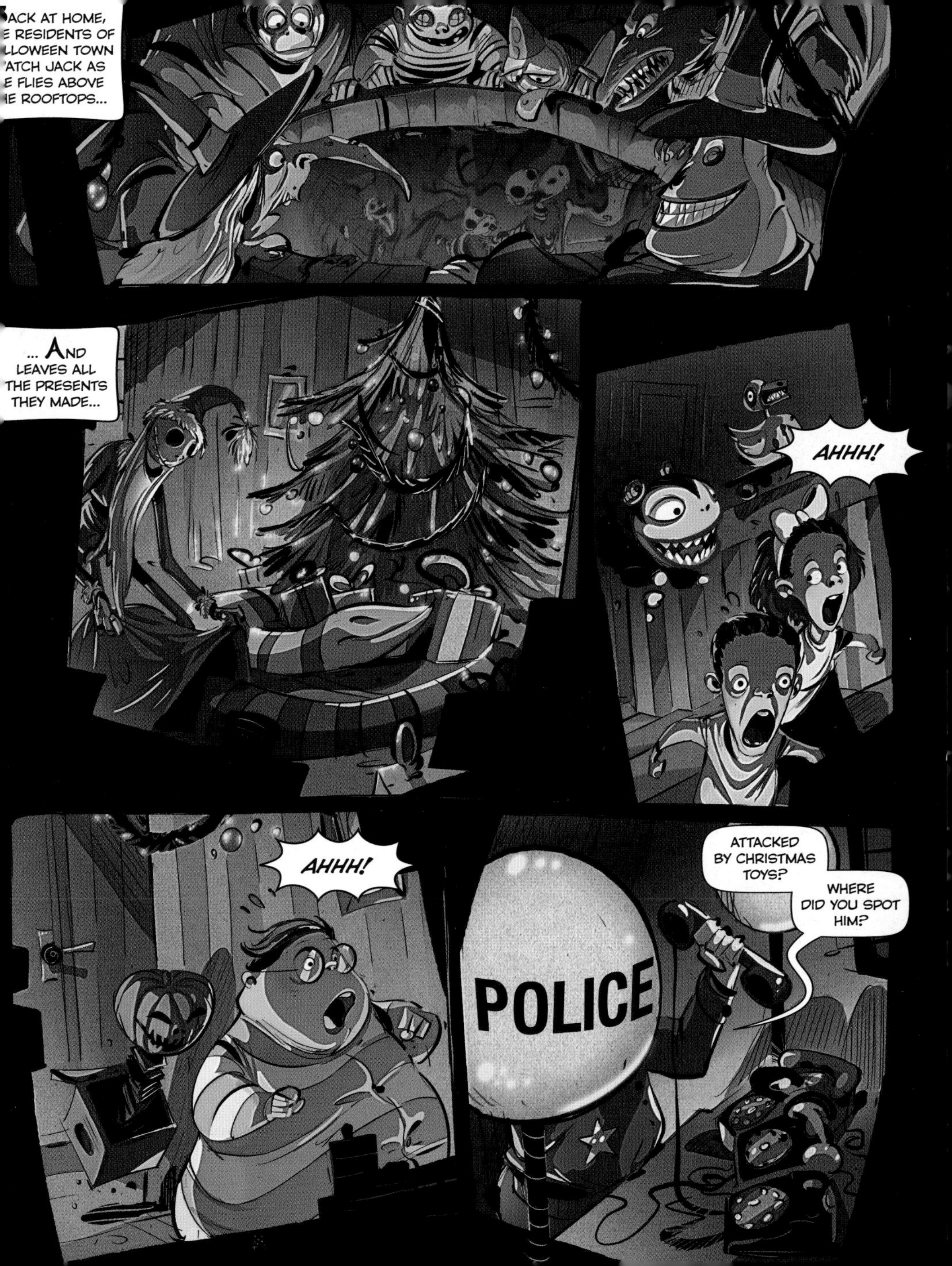
ACK AT HOME,
E RESIDENTS OF
LLOWEEN TOWN
ATCH JACK AS
E FLIES ABOVE
E ROOFTOPS...
... AND LEAVES ALL THE PRESENTS THEY MADE...
AHHH!
AHHH!
POLICE
ATTACKED BY CHRISTMAS TOYS?
WHERE DID YOU SPOT HIM?

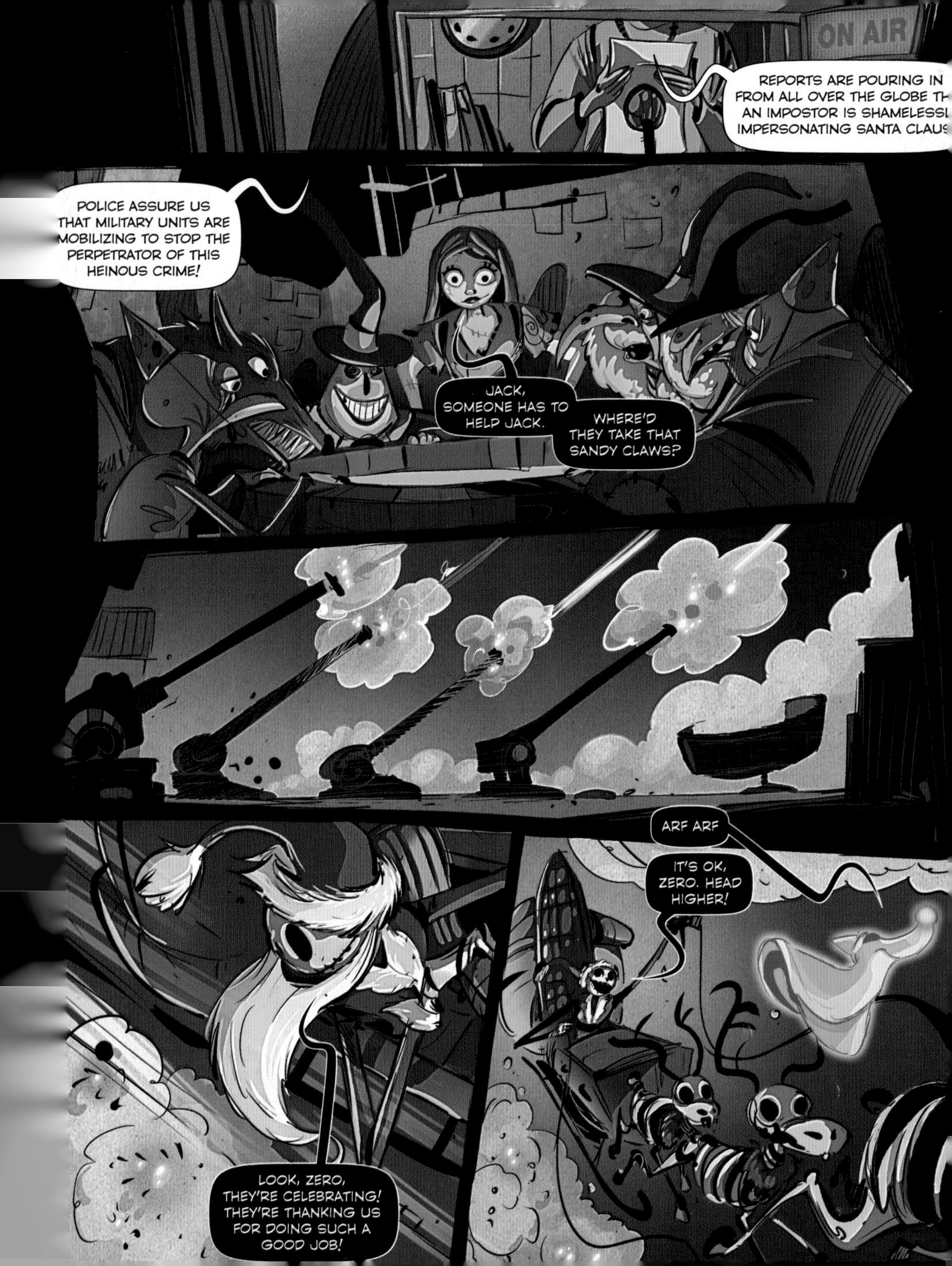
ON AIR
REPORTS ARE POURING IN FROM ALL OVER THE GLOBE TH AN IMPOSTOR IS SHAMELESSL IMPERSONATING SANTA CLAUS
POLICE ASSURE US THAT MILITARY UNITS ARE MOBILIZING TO STOP THE PERPETRATOR OF THIS HEINOUS CRIME!
JACK, SOMEONE HAS TO HELP JACK.
WHERE'D THEY TAKE THAT SANDY CLAWS?
LOOK, ZERO, THEY'RE CELEBRATING! THEY'RE THANKING US FOR DOING SUCH A GOOD JOB!
ARF ARF
IT'S OK, ZERO. HEAD HIGHER!

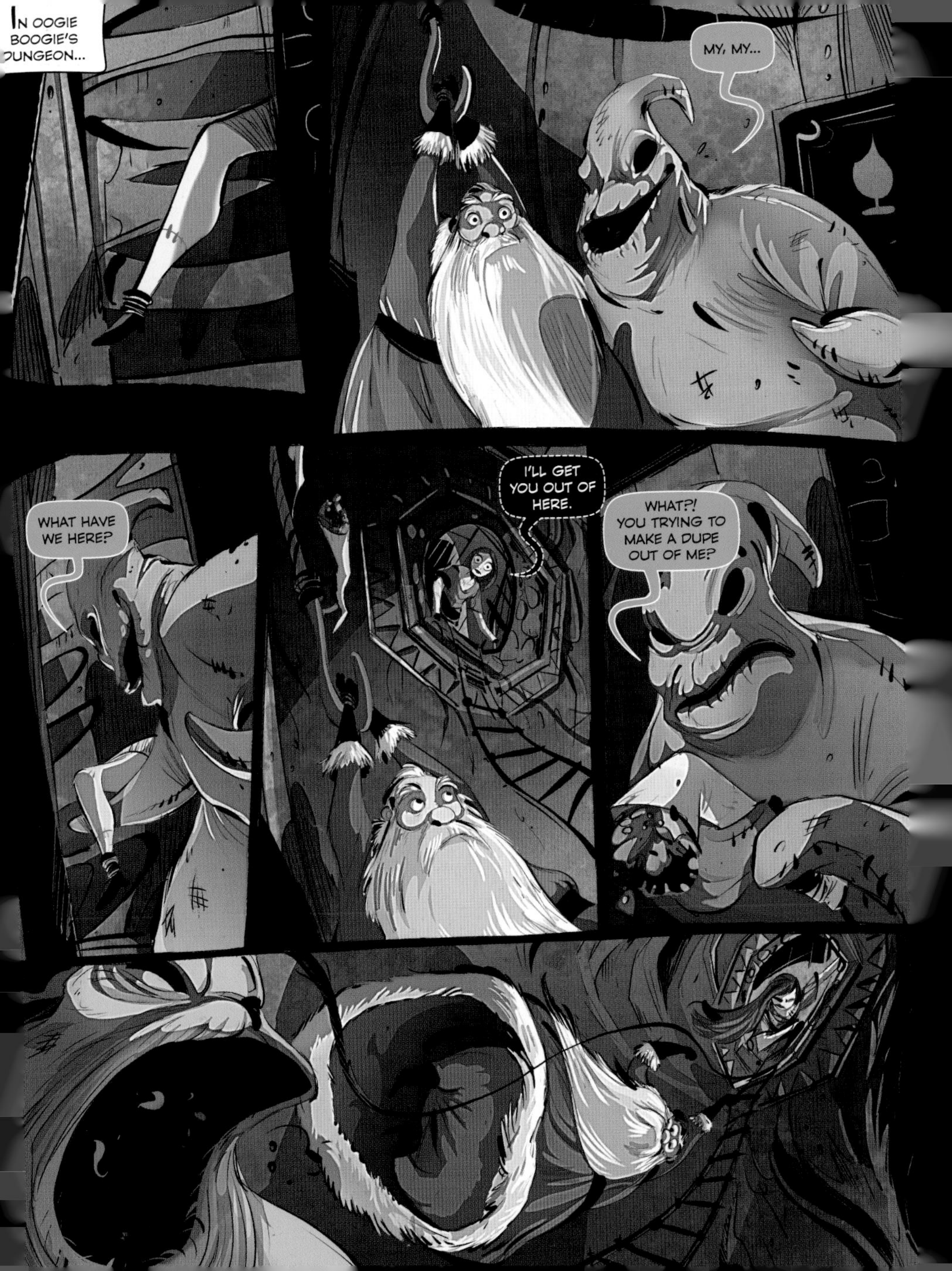
In oogie boogie's dungeon...
My, my...
What have we here?
I'll get you out of here.
What?! You trying to make a dupe out of me?

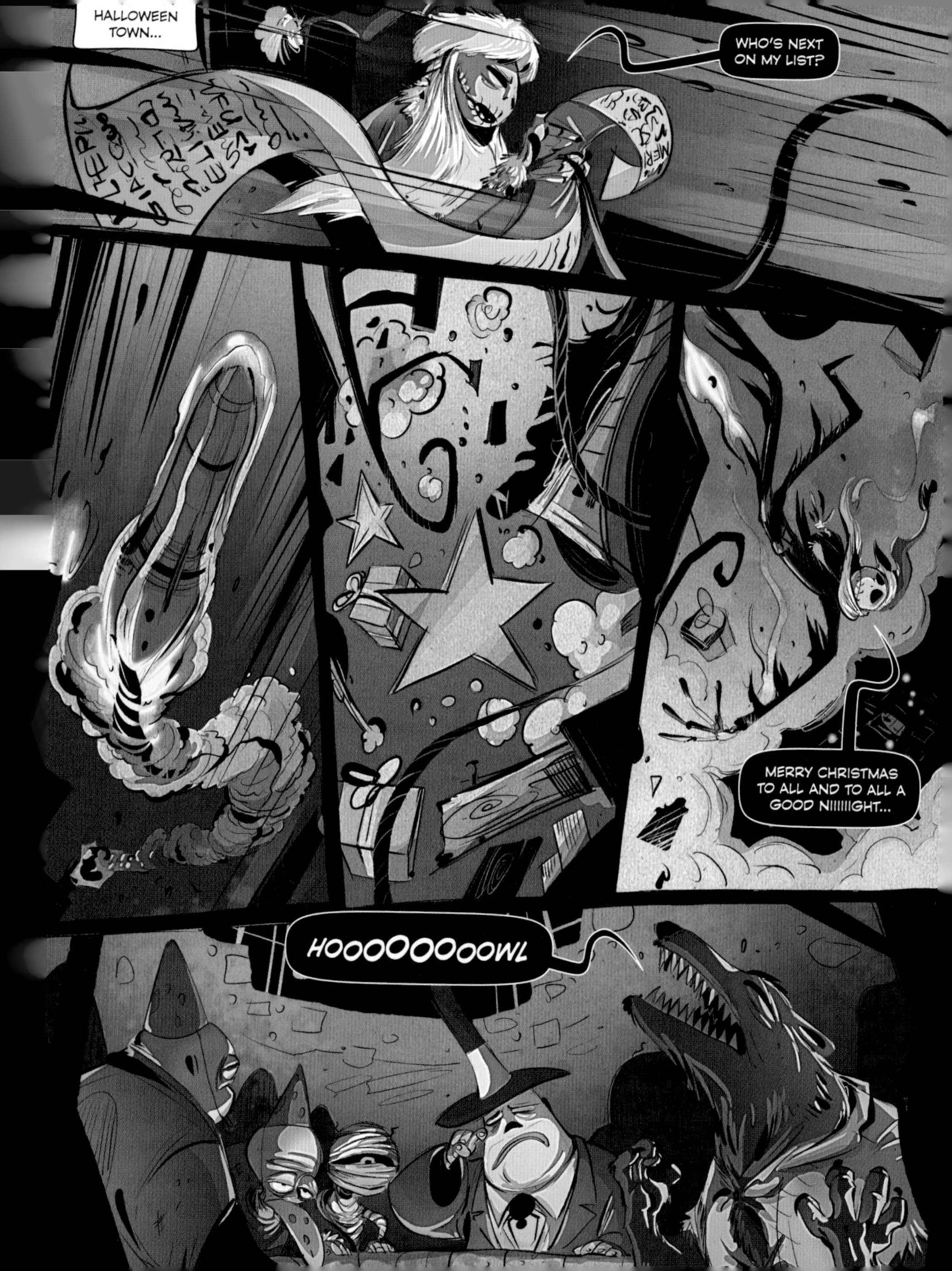
HALLOWEEN TOWN...
WHO'S NEXT ON MY LIST?
MERRY CHRISTMAS TO ALL AND TO ALL A GOOD NIIIIIGHT...
HOOOOOOOOWL

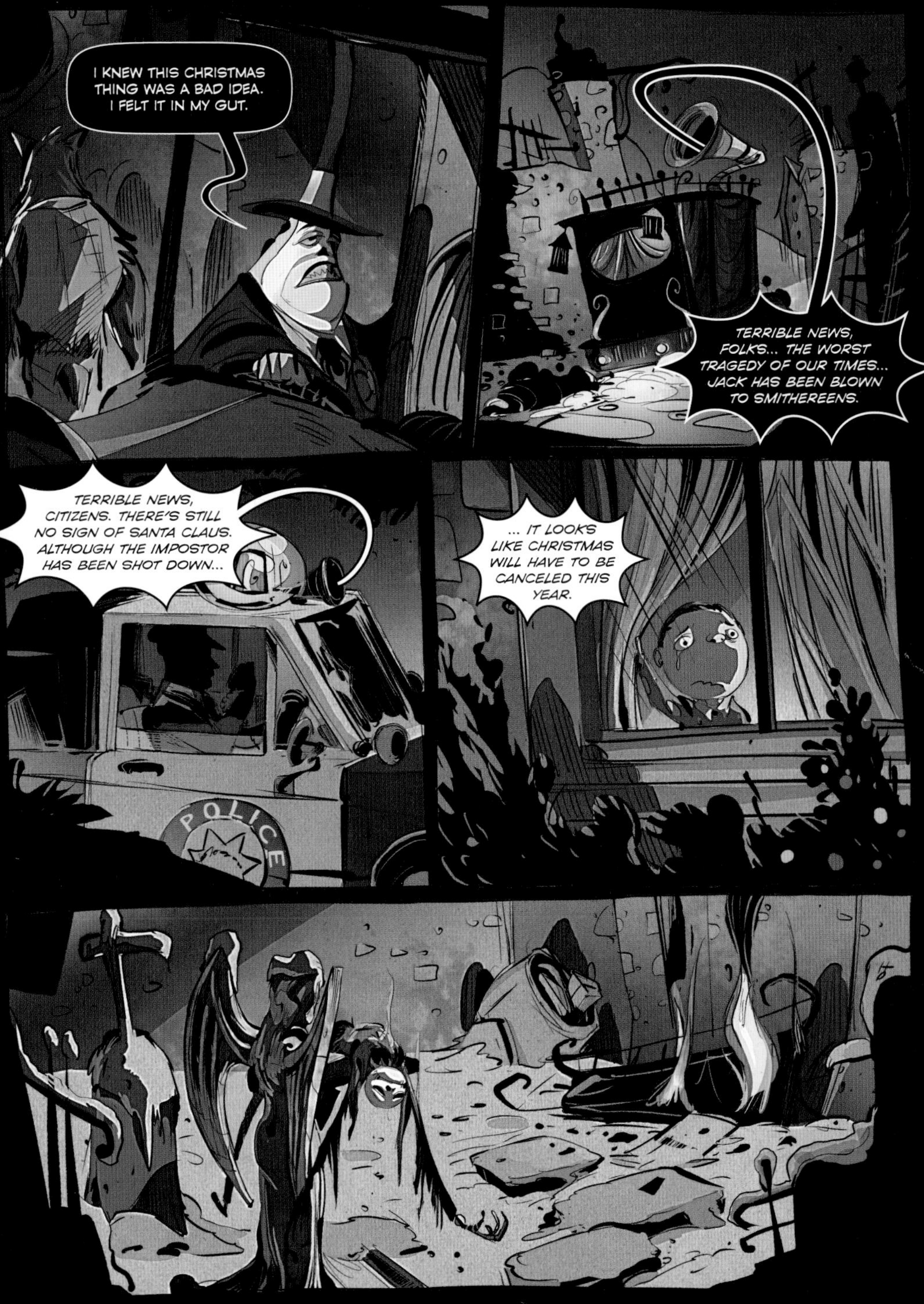
I KNEW THIS CHRISTMAS THING WAS A BAD IDEA. I FELT IT IN MY GUT.
TERRIBLE NEWS, FOLKS... THE WORST TRAGEDY OF OUR TIMES... JACK HAS BEEN BLOWN TO SMITHEREENS.
TERRIBLE NEWS, CITIZENS. THERE'S STILL NO SIGN OF SANTA CLAUS. ALTHOUGH THE IMPOSTOR HAS BEEN SHOT DOWN...
... IT LOOKS LIKE CHRISTMAS WILL HAVE TO BE CANCELED THIS YEAR.
POLICE

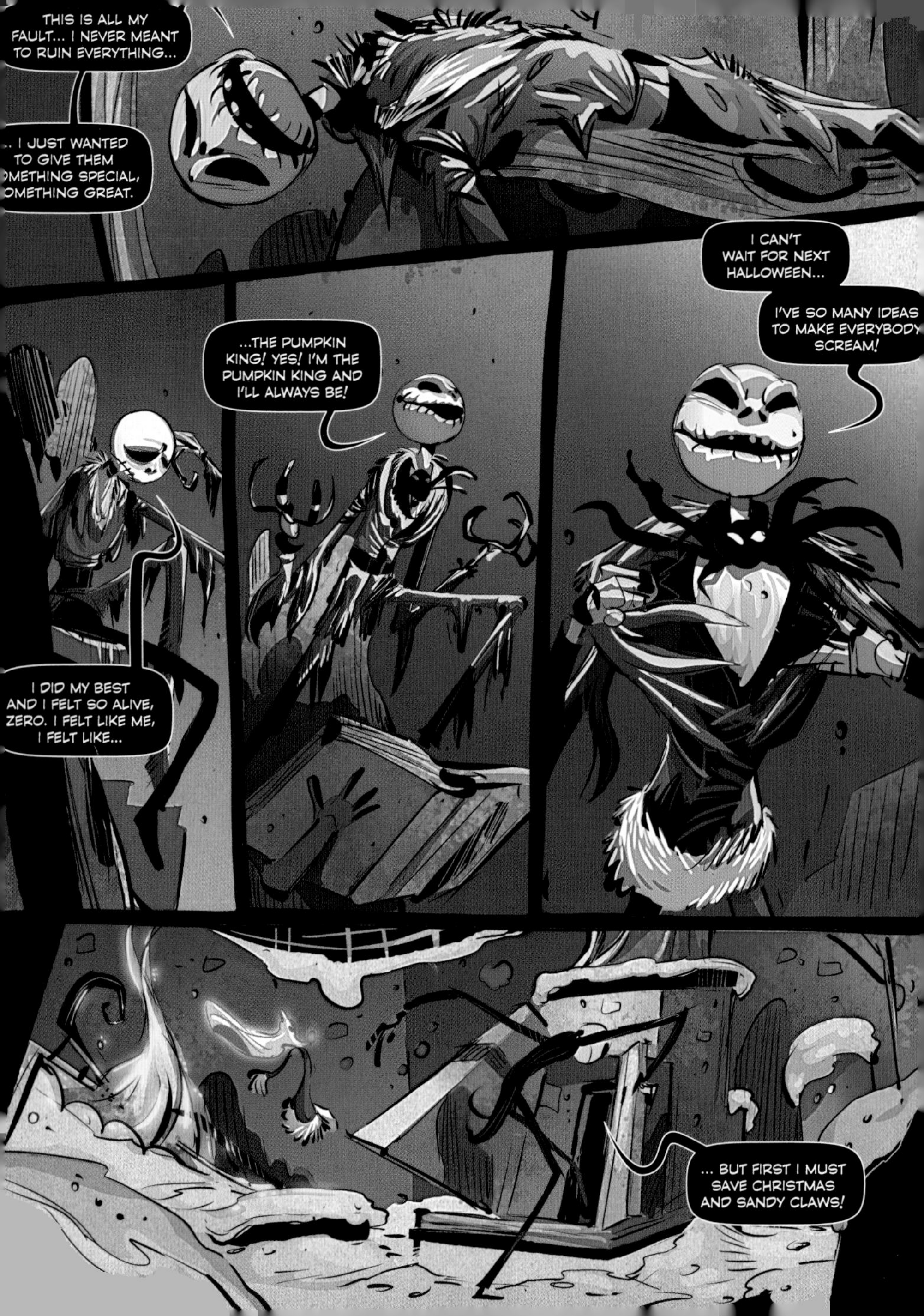
THIS IS ALL MY FAULT... I NEVER MEANT TO RUIN EVERYTHING...
... I JUST WANTED TO GIVE THEM OMETHING SPECIAL, OMETHING GREAT.
I DID MY BEST AND I FELT SO ALIVE, ZERO. I FELT LIKE ME, I FELT LIKE...
...THE PUMPKIN KING! YES! I'M THE PUMPKIN KING AND I'LL ALWAYS BE!
I CAN'T WAIT FOR NEXT HALLOWEEN...
I'VE SO MANY IDEAS TO MAKE EVERYBODY SCREAM!
... BUT FIRST I MUST SAVE CHRISTMAS AND SANDY CLAWS!

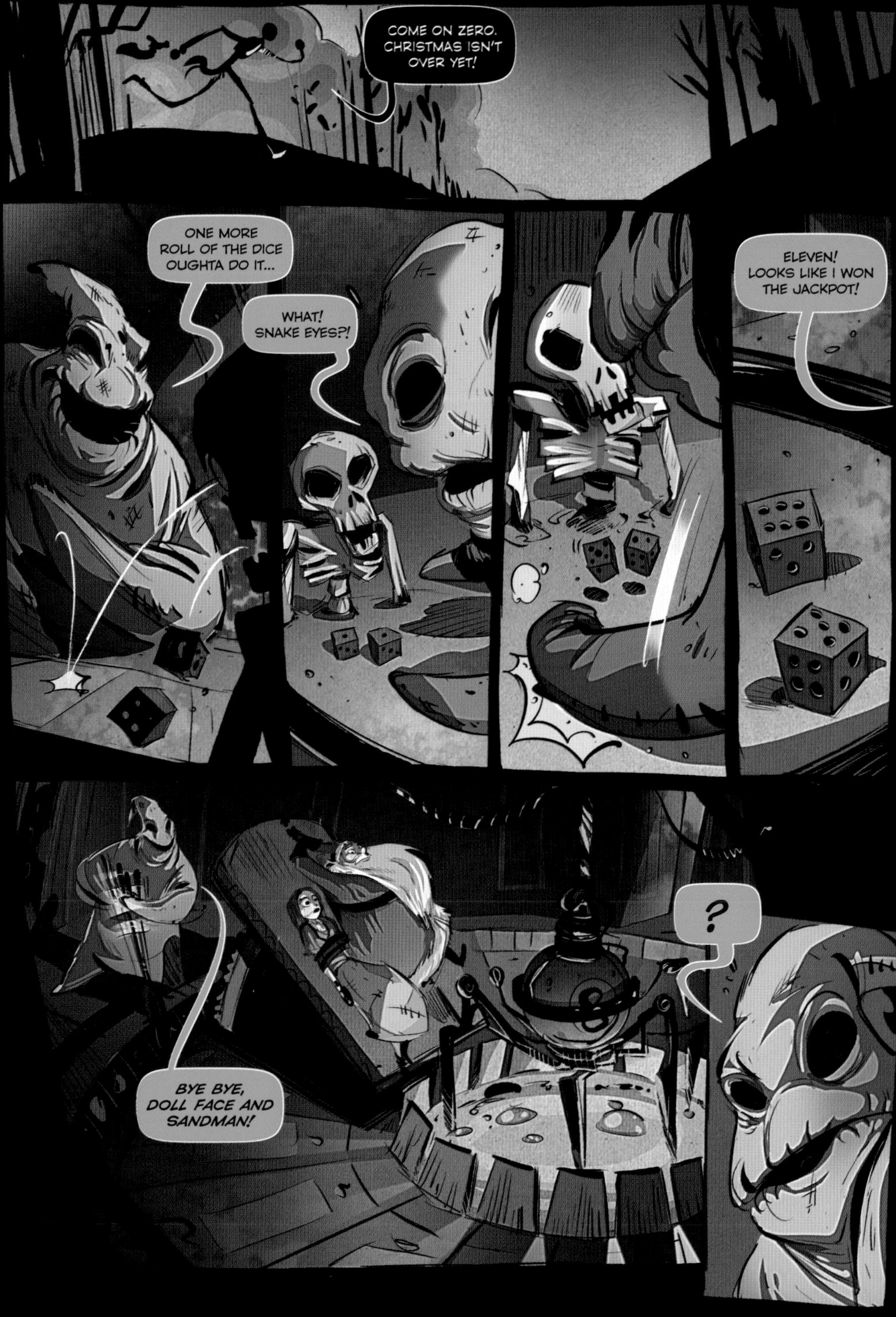
COME ON ZERO. CHRISTMAS ISN'T OVER YET!
ONE MORE ROLL OF THE DICE OUGHTA DO IT...
WHAT! SNAKE EYES?!
ELEVEN! LOOKS LIKE I WON THE JACKPOT!
BYE BYE, DOLL FACE AND SANDMAN!
?

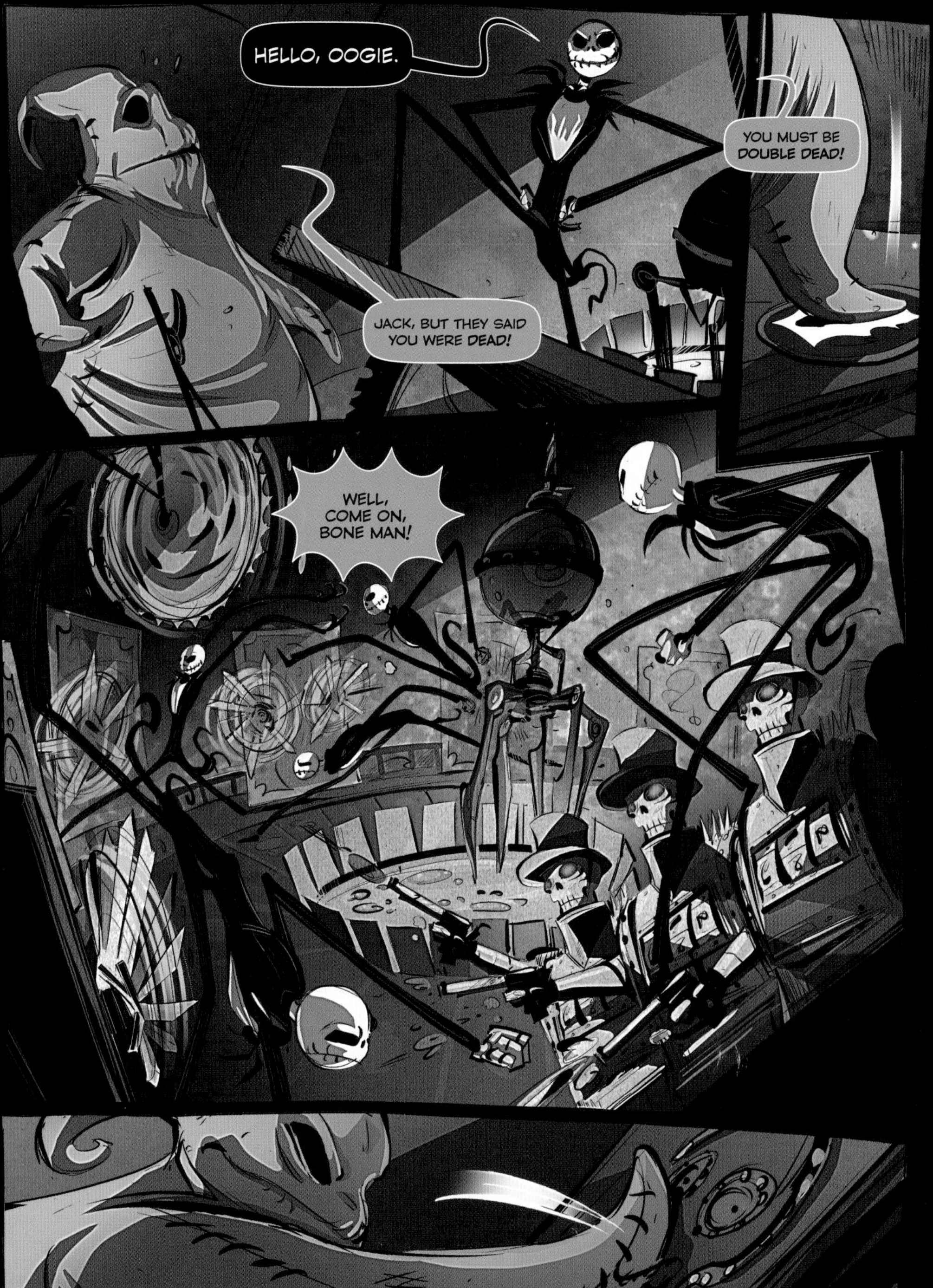
HELLO, OOGIE.
JACK, BUT THEY SAID YOU WERE DEAD!
YOU MUST BE DOUBLE DEAD!
WELL, COME ON, BONE MAN!

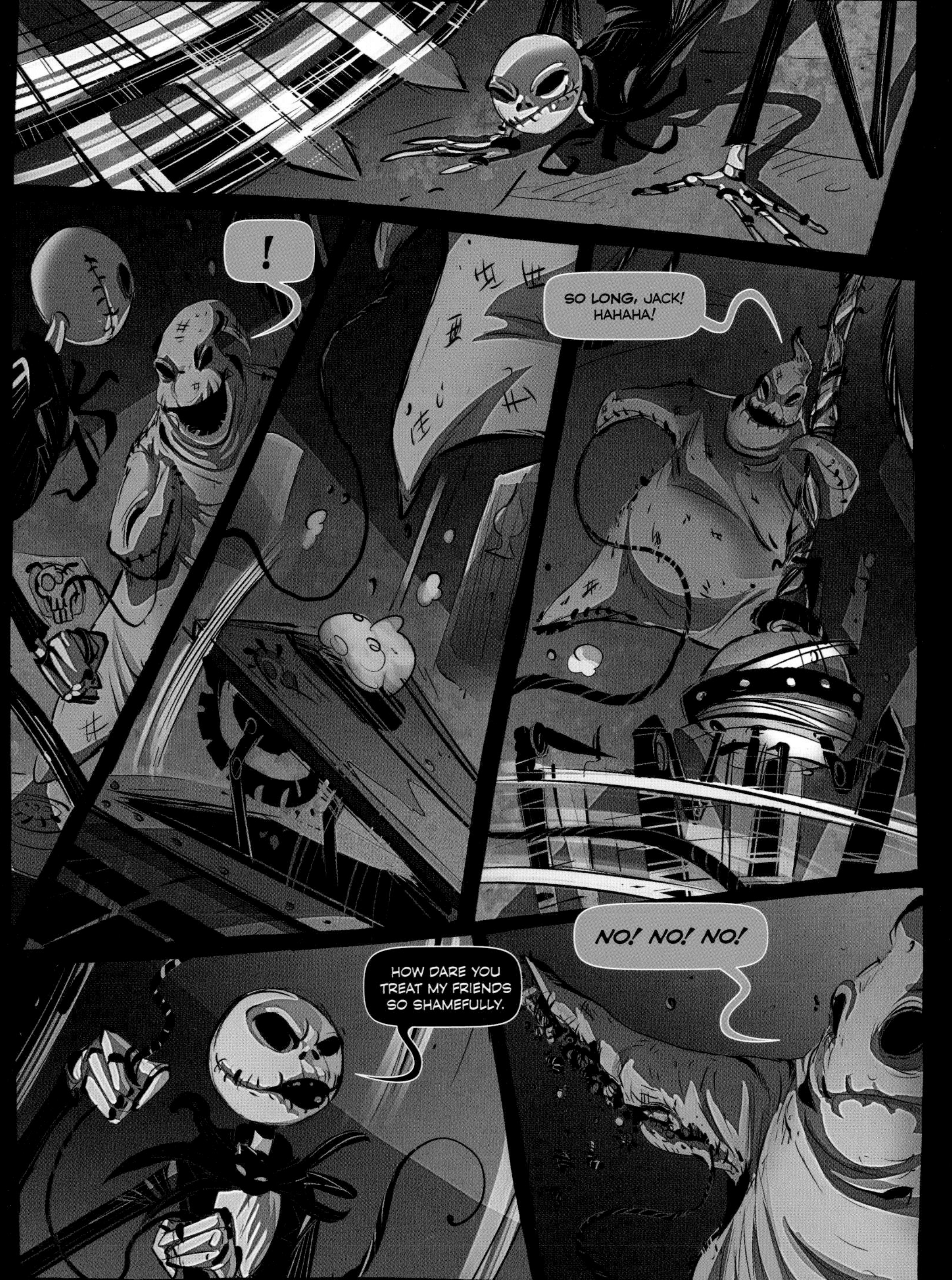
!
SO LONG, JACK! HAHAHA!
NO! NO! NO!
HOW DARE YOU TREAT MY FRIENDS SO SHAMEFULLY.

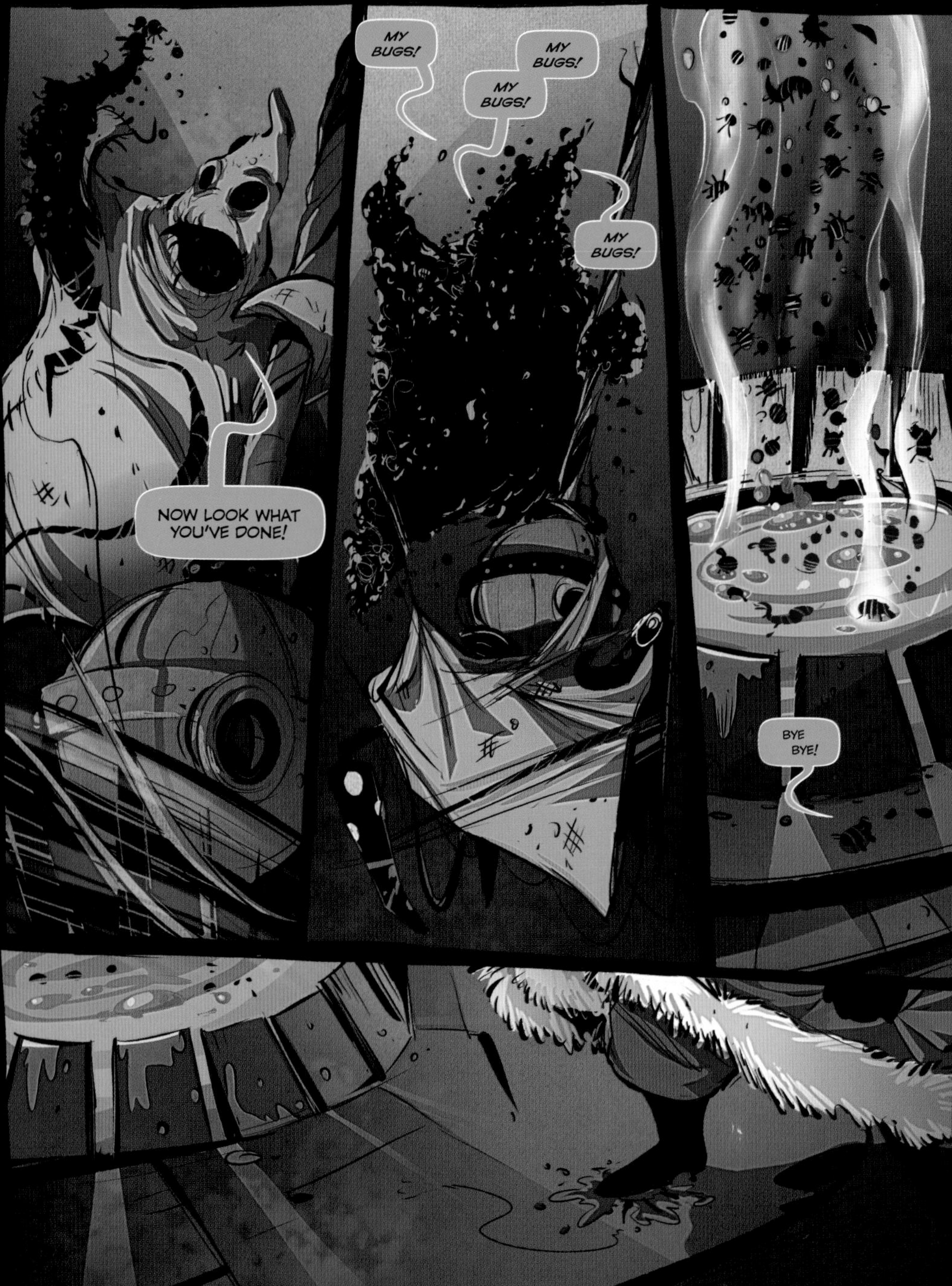
NOW LOOK WHAT YOU'VE DONE!
MY BUGS!
MY BUGS!
MY BUGS!
MY BUGS!
BYE BYE!

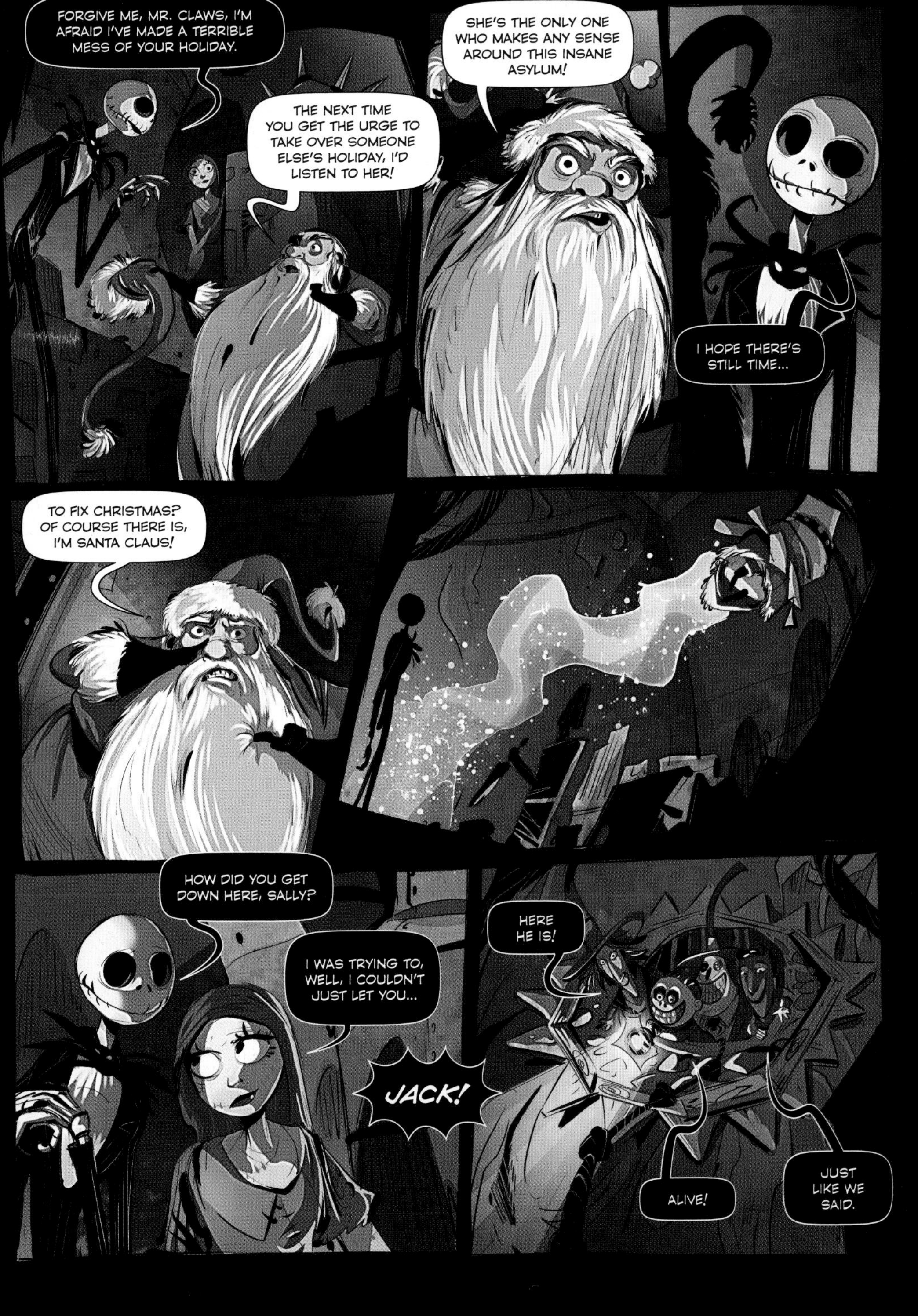
FORGIVE ME, MR. CLAWS, I'M AFRAID I'VE MADE A TERRIBLE MESS OF YOUR HOLIDAY.
THE NEXT TIME YOU GET THE URGE TO TAKE OVER SOMEONE ELSE'S HOLIDAY, I'D LISTEN TO HER!
SHE'S THE ONLY ONE WHO MAKES ANY SENSE AROUND THIS INSANE ASYLUM!
I HOPE THERE'S STILL TIME...
TO FIX CHRISTMAS? OF COURSE THERE IS, I'M SANTA CLAUS!
HOW DID YOU GET DOWN HERE, SALLY?
I WAS TRYING TO, WELL, I COULDN'T JUST LET YOU...
JACK!
HERE HE IS!
ALIVE!
JUST LIKE WE SAID.

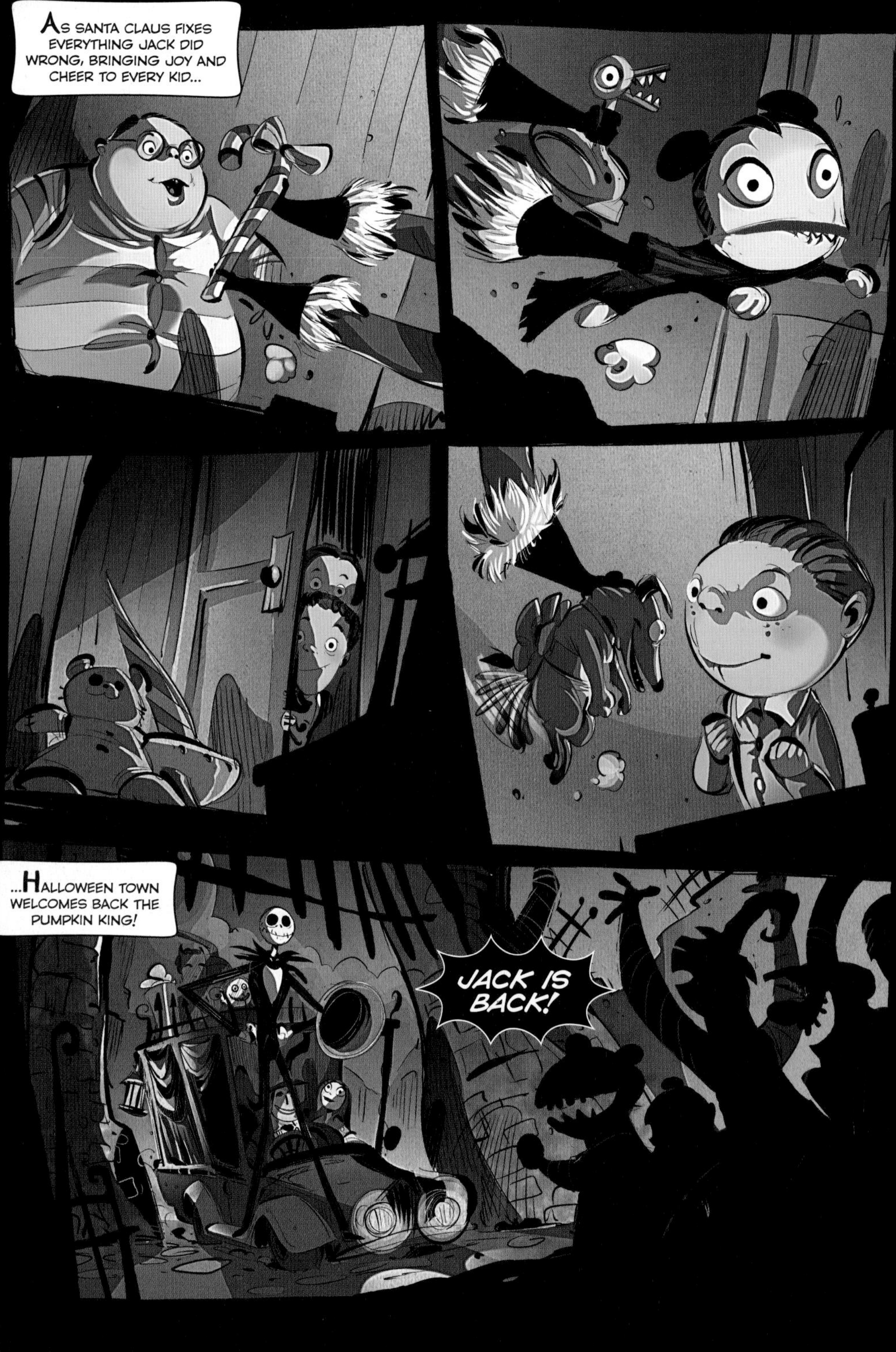
As santa claus fixes everything jack did wrong, bringing joy and cheer to every kid...
...Halloween town welcomes back the pumpkin king!
Jack is back!

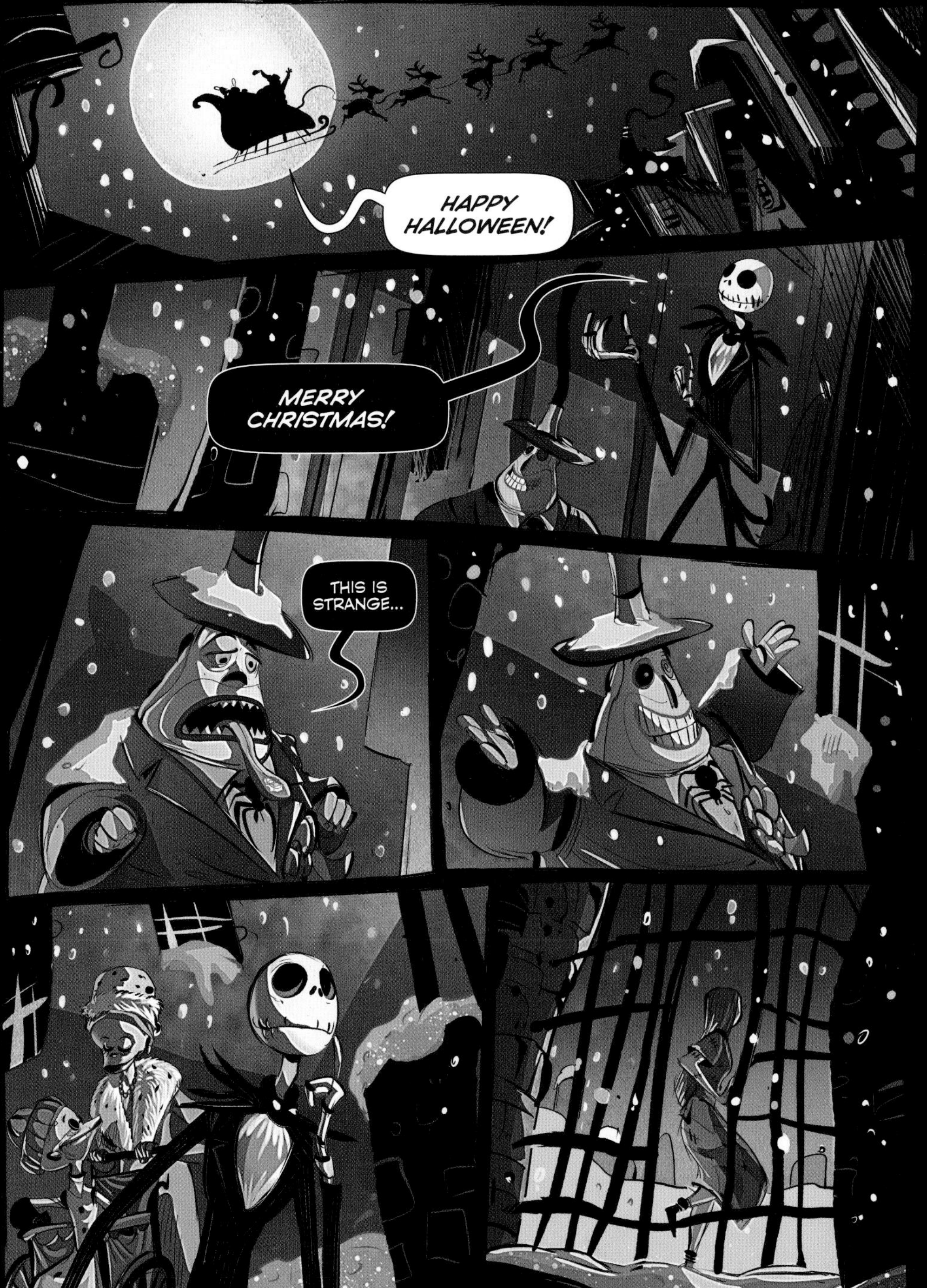
HAPPY HALLOWEEN!
MERRY CHRISTMAS!
THIS IS STRANGE...

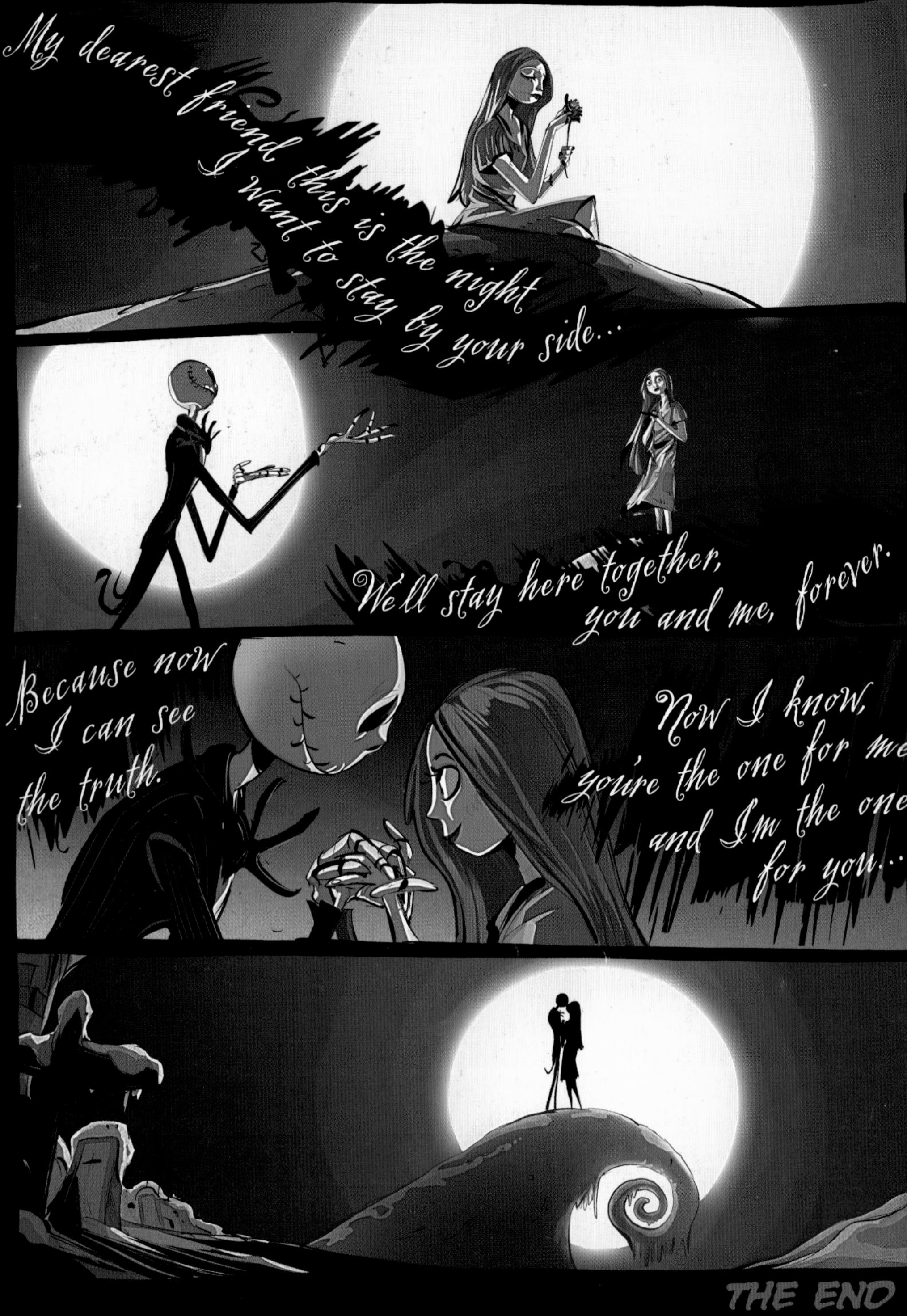
My dearest friend this is the night
I want to stay by your side...
We'll stay here together,
you and me, forever.
Because now
I can see
the truth.
Now I know,
you're the one for me
and I'm the one
for you...
THE END

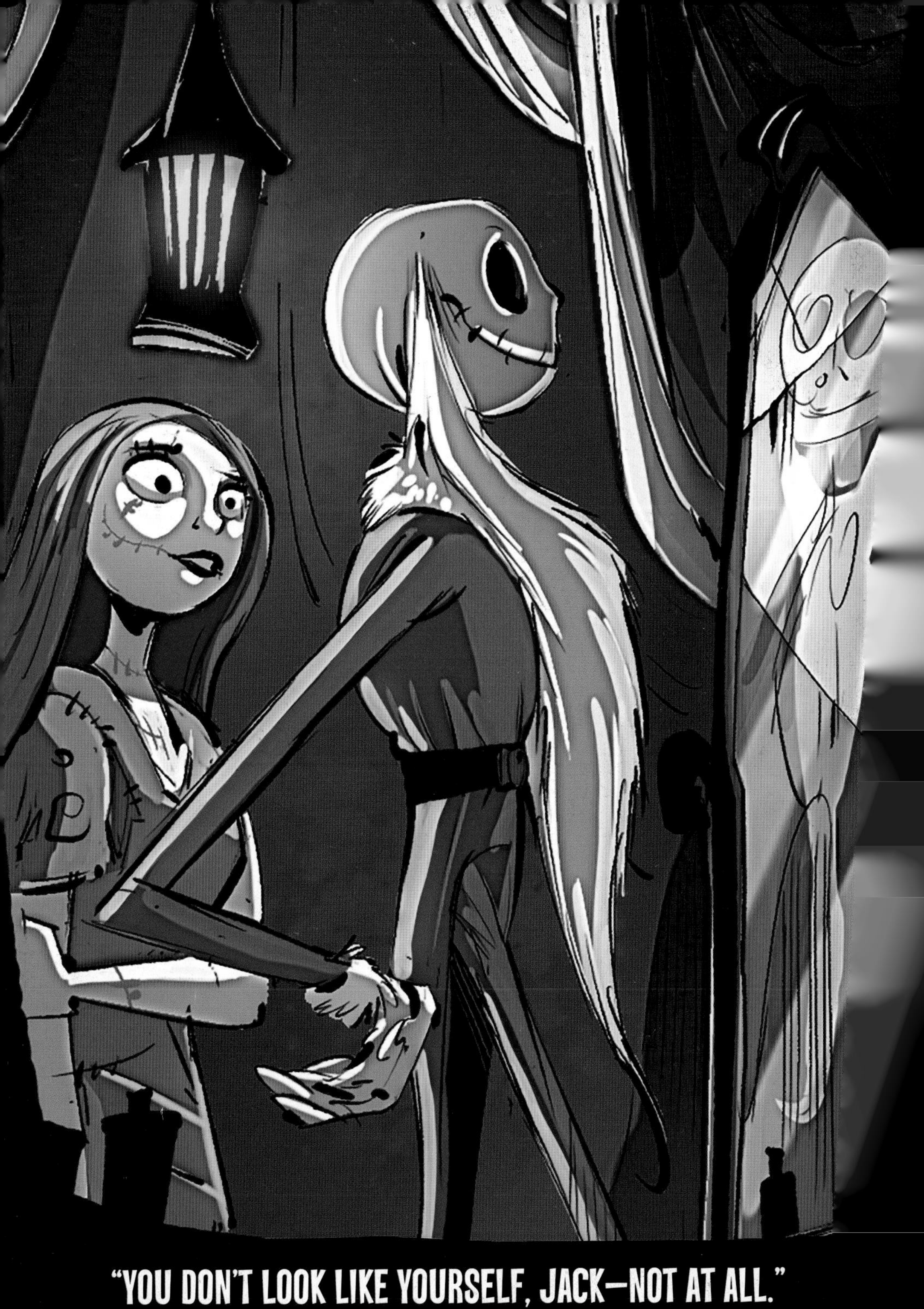

"YOU DON'T LOOK LIKE YOURSELF, JACK—NOT AT ALL."
"IT COULDN'T BE MORE WONDERFUL!"

—SALLY AND JACK

SCRIPT ADAPTATION **ALESSANDRO FERRARI**

LAYOUTS, PENCILS, AND INKS **MASSIMILIANO NARCISCO**

COLOR **KAWAII STUDIO**

LETTERS **EDIZIONI BD**

COVER ART **MASSIMILIANO NARCISCO** WITH COLOR BY **KAWAII STUDIO**

Special thanks to **Tim Burton**, **Dominique Flynn**,
Dale Kennedy, **Caitlin Dodson**, and **Albert Park**.

DARK HORSE BOOKS
President and Publisher **Mike Richardson**
Collection Editor **Freddye Miller**
Collection Assistant Editor **Judy Khuu**
Collection Designer **Anita Magaña**
Digital Art Technician **Allyson Haller**

Neil Hankerson Executive Vice President, **Tom Weddle** Chief Financial Officer, **Randy Stradley** Vice President of Publishing, **Nick McWhorter** Chief Business Development Officer, **Dale LaFountain** Chief Information Officer, **Matt Parkinson** Vice President of Marketing, **Vanessa Todd-Holmes** Vice President of Production and Scheduling, **Mark Bernardi** Vice President of Book Trade and Digital Sales, **Ken Lizzi** General Counsel, **Dave Marshall** Editor in Chief, **Davey Estrada** Editorial Director, **Chris Warner** Senior Books Editor, **Cary Grazzini** Director of Specialty Projects, **Lia Ribacchi** Art Director, **Matt Dryer** Director of Digital Art and Prepress, **Michael Gombos** Senior Director of Licensed Publications, **Kari Yadro** Director of Custom Programs, **Kari Torson** Director of International Licensing, **Sean Brice** Director of Trade Sales

DISNEY PUBLISHING WORLDWIDE GLOBAL MAGAZINES, COMICS AND PARTWORKS
PUBLISHER **Lynn Waggoner** • EDITORIAL TEAM **Bianca Coletti** (Director, Magazines), **Guido Frazzini** (Director, Comics), **Carlotta Quattrocolo** (Executive Editor), **Stefano Ambrosio** (Executive Editor, New IP), **Camilla Vedove** (Senior Manager, Editorial Development), **Behnoosh Khalili** (Senior Editor), **Julie Dorris** (Senior Editor), **Mina Riazi** (Assistant Editor), **Gabriela Capasso** (Assistant Editor) • DESIGN **Enrico Soave** (Senior Designer) • ART **Ken Shue** (VP, Global Art), **Manny Mederos** (Senior Illustration Manager, Comics and Magazines), **Roberto Santillo** (Creative Director), **Marco Ghiglione** (Creative Manager), **Stefano Attardi** (Illustration Manager) • PORTFOLIO MANAGEMENT **Olivia Ciancarelli** (Director) • BUSINESS & MARKETING **Mariantonietta Galla** (Senior Manager, Franchise), **Virpi Korhonen** (Editorial Manager)

Disney Tim Burton's The Nightmare Before Christmas: The Story of the Movie in Comics

Published by Dark Horse Books
A division of Dark Horse Comics LLC
10956 SE Main Street
Milwaukie, OR 97222
DarkHorse.com

To find a comics shop in your area, visit comicshoplocator.com

First Dark Horse Books edition: August 2020
Ebook ISBN 978-1-50671-751-7
Hardcover ISBN 978-1-50671-742-5

1 3 5 7 9 10 8 6 4 2
Printed in China